WHISKING
up
WHODUNITS

Eliza Floretta

Copyright © 2025 by Eliza Floretta

All rights reserved.

No portion of this book may be reproduced in any form without written permission from the publisher or author, except as permitted by U.S. copyright law.

Cover art by Liz Pauly

Contents

Sign up for my Newsletter   1

Dedication   2

1. Chapter One   3
2. Chapter Two   13
3. Chapter Three   17
4. Chapter Four   26
5. Chapter Five   34
6. Chapter Six   42
7. Chapter Seven   47
8. Chapter Eight   52
9. Chapter Nine   62
10. Chapter Ten   68
11. Chapter Eleven   75
12. Chapter Twelve   82
13. Chapter Thirteen   89

14.	Chapter Fourteen	95
15.	Chapter Fifteen	101
16.	Chapter Sixteen	104
17.	Chapter Seventeen	107
18.	Chapter Eighteen	110
19.	Chapter Nineteen	116
20.	Chapter Twenty	121
21.	Chapter Twenty-One	128
22.	Chapter Twenty-Two	131
23.	Chapter Twenty-Three	134
24.	Chapter Twenty-Four	140
25.	Chapter Twenty-Five	145
26.	Chapter Twenty-Six	150
27.	Chapter Twenty-Seven	155
28.	Chapter Twenty-Eight	165
29.	Chapter Twenty-Nine	178
30.	Chapter Thirty	187
31.	Chapter Thirty-One	193
32.	Chapter Thirty-Two	196
33.	Chapter Thirty-Three	199

34. Chapter Thirty-Four	206
About the Author	211

Sign up for my Newsletter

Please consider signing up for my newsletter at https://authorelizafloretta.com/ for free mystery stories (that I plan to give away in the near future), and to be the first to hear about free book promos, sales, and future releases.

I really appreciate my readers so much! You help make my dreams a reality. I cannot thank you enough for giving a no-name author like me a chance on your shelf.

Feel free to reach out through social media. I love hearing from readers!

Instagram: @ElizaFloretta_Author
TikTok: @ElizaFloretta_Author
Facebook: Author Eliza Floretta

Dedicated to my grandmother, who loved cozy mysteries. I wish you could've read this story.

Chapter One

The oven breathed hot air on Emma as she slid a tray of cookies onto the metal. She sighed as her glasses fogged up, a usual occurrence. "Exactly the look I'm going for—blind baker," she muttered, wiping them on her apron.

Amber, perched on a stool, chewed the chain of her necklace like it was a piece of gum, something she often did when anxious or bored. "You know, you're the only person I'd wake up for at this hour. The sun's not even up, but here I am, ready to supervise." She grinned, the creases of her cheeks showing off her heavy application of concealer.

Emma rolled her eyes. "Yeah, okay, Miss Supervisor. I'll pretend I don't know the real reason you're here this early." Which was that Amber's insomnia was in high-gear, and she needed a distraction.

"Are you going to help or just sit there?" Emma asked, taking a tray of hot cookies from the second oven.

"Sit here." Amber smiled coyly. "And admire you." She leaned in to examine the cookies, the scent of vanilla and chocolate wafting off them. "You know I fantasize about cooking up beautiful meals like you do. I think I'll be able to relax and create something splendidly delicious but then comes reality. I'm over here overwhelmed and irritable because my kitchen is a mess, and there's no room for me to work. The oven's aggravating my menopause, and my husband's just about had enough, so he forbids me from ever cooking again and orders a pizza or comes here for a meal, you know." She laughed, fanning herself with her hands. "Even just watching you stresses me out sometimes."

Emma rolled her eyes. "You are so dramatic."

Amber shrugged. "I'm just honest." She looked toward the door that showed off Emma's wild garden—a mix of flowers, herbs, and an array of vegetables. "I heard your granddaughter is arriving today. How old is she now? Eleven?"

"Sixteen," Emma corrected.

"Sixteen? Wow, I blink and there goes years." She wiped the saliva on her necklace onto her shirt collar. "I suppose you talked to your daughter to arrange it?"

"Only briefly." Emma's fingers clenched her dirty apron.

"So, she sends you her mini-me, but won't come visit herself?" Amber's tone was critical.

"Bella's busy. She's a single mom now and running her own business baking cakes."

"Well, I suppose she can't hate you that much if she's followed in your footsteps." Amber shrugged and dabbed her red-stained lips with a napkin.

Emma sighed and went to sit across from her friend. She drew a line across the flour-dusted counter with her finger. "Maybe."

"You weren't a bad mother, you know," Amber said. "She's just a brat." She pushed back her graying hair as she looked toward the large arched windows that oversaw Lake Erie. "It's a generational thing, you know. All these kids growing up, forgetting their parents. My kids aren't much better."

"They at least make time to come visit," Emma reminded, pouring two cups of freshly brewed coffee from her French press. "Your son, Thomas, lives all the way out in BC, so he has an excuse. My daughter's just in Toronto. It's not far."

"Anne's daughter practically lives next door, and hardly makes time to visit, even still."

Emma thought of Anne. The old lady was a bit sour, so Emma couldn't blame her daughter for avoiding her. Emma avoided her, too, and dreaded when she came by for one of her famous muffins. "I just don't know where I went wrong with this whole parenting thing." She took the saucer of cream to the lip of her cup and poured it in, watching the white swirl around the black—a tornado of frothing waves against a dark backdrop.

"At least everything else in your life has gone well. Your husband is still positively smitten, and your cozy little business is the talk of Canada. Why, I even saw it mentioned in a headline on the Albertian Cooking Blog." Amber's dazzling smile lifted her high cheekbones. "They raved about your heart-melting muffins made with real butter and zero seed oils!"

Emma laughed. "I'll probably get sued for causing heart-attacks next." Emma took a sip of her coffee, ignoring the bitterness collecting at the pit of her stomach. Maybe it needed a dash more cream.

A warm breeze blew through a partially open window. Emma got up to close it, the old floorboards creaking at every step. She wasn't sure why she wanted to close it—maybe just to distract herself from the conversation at hand. It had been years since she had seen her daughter. Years. And she couldn't ignore how broken such a fact made her feel.

Amber waved her hand. "Leave it open, will ya? I enjoy listening to the waves. Lived here my whole life and can't get enough."

From the window, Emma noticed Tim's truck entering the parking lot. He got out, came around the front of his car, and opened the passenger door. Chloe slid out of the seat; a pink purse swung over her shoulder. She wore jeans and a t-shirt, her straight, blonde hair reaching to her mid-back.

"They're here early," Amber said, peering over Emma's shoulder. "He would've had to leave here at what? Two?"

"Yeah, well, I need Tim's help with the guests. I can't do everything."

"You have me."

Emma smiled. Amber was a great friend, but her customer service skills were desperately lacking.

Every time she tried to help, it ended in disaster. She was just too blunt for her own good.

"You really should hire more help," Amber said. "I know you don't trust anyone, but this place is getting too busy for you to keep up your one-woman show. Sooner or later, you're going to have to stop wearing all the shoes. Silvia agrees with me. You remember Silvia?"

"Of course. I still talk with her on the phone every couple of weeks. Nothing could break our gang up, not even a ridiculous distance."

"Crazy to think it's been over forty years since our senior prom. Those were the days." Amber's chest rose as she let out a long sigh.

Before Emma could respond, Tim walked through the backdoor into the kitchen. He dropped Chloe's luggage by the doormat. "Sorry, I was hoping to get here sooner, but we had to make some pit-stops."

"Because I'm sure Chloe just loved getting up at three a.m. to make it here before the guests woke up." Amber smiled at the girl as she walked through the door.

Chloe shrugged. "I slept on the drive." She hung her purse on a hook and looked over at her grandmother. "Hi, Granny Em."

"Chloe, it's so good to see you." Emma was about to wrap her lanky arms around the girl, but stopped when she remembered the flour on her apron. "Sorry, I only just finished baking."

Chloe looked at her apron. "It's okay. I'm not much of a hugger."

"I'll help you get settled while Granny Em gets things ready to go." Tim lifted the luggage, his muscles flexing under his plaid shirt. Emma smiled at him as he brushed past her, and he smiled back.

Four decades, and he still made her heart skip a beat like they were teenagers again.

"The way you look at him." Amber laughed, gripping Emma by the shoulder.

Emma blushed. She remembered how Amber had yelled across the bleachers that her friend liked the quarterback number twenty-five. Emma nearly fainted from embarrassment, but in the end everything worked out. "I have you to thank."

"Yes, you do."

It wasn't until late evening that the bed-and-breakfast finally quieted down. Emma hung up her dirty apron and stepped outside, making her way to the fire pit at the center of the property. There, Amber and her husband, Alexander, sat alongside Chloe and Tim, the firelight casting a warm glow over their faces.

"Took you long enough," Amber scolded. The plate in front of her was empty and at her feet. She caressed a half-full wine glass and leaned against her husband's thick frame.

Alexander wrapped one arm around Amber, making her appear much more petite than she really was. He was a tall man and had once been quite fit during his time in the Royal Canadian Navy, but since retirement, he had packed on the pounds.

"The guests would've understood," Tim said, looking over at Chloe, who was staring absentmindedly toward the fire. "Not every day your granddaughter is visiting."

"I have an image to uphold." Emma took a seat beside her granddaughter and touched her back. "I'm sorry I kept you all waiting."

"Your plate's cold now," Tim said, placing it in his wife's lap.

Emma knew it wasn't. It should've been, but it was far too warm tonight for anything to get cold.

"Thank you." She picked at her butter-drenched potatoes, barely tasting them. The fire crackled, its bright orange glow illuminating the small circle of brown logs and casting flickering shadows against the towering cypress trees. Beyond that, darkness pressed in, the sliver of moon barely a scratch of white in the night sky.

Slowly, everyone started to leave. Chloe was exhausted from the drive here. Tim would help her get settled. Amber and Alexander needed to prep for an event they were planning to host tomorrow. Emma stayed, still poking at some food on her plate. She was so tired, her body ached from head to toe. 'That's what getting old feels like,' her husband often told her. Emma remembered days when she couldn't feel the weight so keenly, when she could run on just a few hours of sleep and still get everything done to perfection.

"Murder's a strong word." The words were whispered but as loud as a siren to Emma.

She lowered her plate to the grass and headed toward the voice. It had come from behind the shed that faced the lake.

Laughter rang out. "I said I'd like to." It was a woman's voice; one Emma couldn't quite pin a name on. "Not that I would, though it's tempting. He led me on, you know. I should've seen it coming. He's the richest man in town and the most conceited jerk and there was no way he'd hurt his reputation by leaving his wife, but…" The woman sighed dramatically.

A twig broke under Emma's feet, sending a loud snap that caused the voices to halt. It wasn't her business to be listening in. Clearly, they weren't discussing actual murder. All her guests were safe. Hopefully, she was too.

If they saw her, this could hurt her reputation far more than neglecting her guests at dinnertime. No one would want to stay at an inn where a nosy woman ran the place.

Emma looked behind her and considered running to the back door. It's not like they'd be able to see her in the dark. But if she entered through the back, it would be obvious who she was. The kitchen was off-limits to the guests.

"Did you hear something?" The woman's voice was unsteady.

"Probably a squirrel."

A soft jingling followed—a bracelet brushing against the shed. Then, a hesitant sigh.

"Well...what do you think? Is there still hope? Do you think he'll come back to me?"

"I think he favors his position far too much," the other voice said. "You're trying to cling to an intangible breeze."

"But, if I can't have him..." There's a muffled sob.

Emma made use of the noisy tears and took off running. She didn't head straight to the door. Instead, she hid behind the cypress tree nearby and watched for heads peeking out from behind the shed, but all was still.

After several minutes, she went inside. The air-conditioned kitchen was cool on her sweaty skin. She reached for the light switch, but thought better of it, just in case.

A million thoughts whizzed through her busy mind. *I wonder who they were talking about.* There were only a few wealthy families in town, Amber and her husband being the richest. *Could it be...* She shook her head. Alexander having an affair was impossible. Amber got on his nerves more often than Emma could count, but they had been together as long as Emma and Tim had, and they seemed happy enough. Alexander had draped his arm across Amber at dinnertime. Usually, men having affairs were distant and cold. Weren't they? Emma wouldn't know. Such a thing was not a common occurrence in this small town. Here, people still prioritized traditional values.

The light turned on, startling her.

"You okay? You look like you've seen a ghost." Tim laughed. "I had expected you to come in sooner. I've been waiting in bed for a while."

Emma forced a smile. "You could've just gone to sleep."

"You know I can't sleep without making sure you're safe."

"What would happen to me, Tim? We don't exactly live in a bad part of town, and I'm not that old."

"Who knows what type of guests we have here?" He walked past her and slid the bolt into place on the back door. His hand lingered on the lock as he turned back to her with a small smile. "But you're probably right. Still, I sleep better knowing you're close."

Emma hooked her arm with his. Looking into his chestnut eyes, she wondered how she'd feel to learn he was having an affair. Not that she had to worry about that, but still. What a blow that would be! That poor woman...

And what if it was Amber who was being cheated on?

Chapter Two

Chloe sat on a Persian rug, facing the antique Victorian dresser with her suitcase by her lap. Her belongings lay in piles around her. She gathered the clothes and began stuffing them into the wood drawers. The musty scent nearly suffocated her as she slid them open. Everything was old and smelt old too, like the pages of a 1900s book.

She slammed the drawers shut and went over to curl up on the windowsill. It was boring as heck here, but at least the lake was beautiful, just as she remembered. Everything was the same as when she'd last visited at ten, before her parents' divorce. Granny Em was always distracted by the cooking and socializing that came with running a B&B, so Chloe could explore to her heart's content without anybody noticing. She found so many hidden compartments in the old home—bookcases that opened to secret rooms, linings on the stairs that slid off, wallpaper that could be pulled apart to reveal a secret cove and then rolled back over.

Chloe loved playing detective. Her mother claimed it's what she had in common with her grandmother, not that Chloe would know. She hardly knew Granny Em, just as she hardly knew her mother. They were both far too busy to notice her unless she was getting into trouble, of course. Then all eyes were glued to her.

It's why her mother sent her away.

She was just a ball of yarn spreading trouble wherever she went.

It's what Mom deserved, Chloe inwardly groaned. Just because it was the biggest event of her career didn't give her any right to forget my birthday.

But she had forgotten, and Chloe had had enough. She was tired of being invisible, so she sabotaged it—all of it. Maybe her mother's livelihood was forever trashed, as she claimed, and they'd have to move in with the homeless while they waited five years for subsidized housing to open up.

That threat had fallen on empty ears, though. Chloe wasn't afraid of sleeping in a cardboard box; she was afraid of staying invisible. And being here wouldn't have been so bad, except she was invisible here, too, just a ghost that was spotted only intermittently.

A knock came at the door. Chloe didn't budge.

"May I come in?" Pops asked.

"I'm dressed, don't worry."

"Uhm, okay." Pops cleared his throat as he slowly opened the door. "I was wondering if you wanted to help me run this place. Some rooms need to be cleaned and I'll have to weed the garden before Granny Em notices I've neglected it."

"I'd rather not."

"I'll pay you a little something. It won't be so bad. We could listen to that music you like and Granny Em could whip us up some homemade ice cream when we're done."

"No, thanks." Chloe slid off the windowsill. "I think the lake's calling my name." She rummaged through her suitcase and pulled out a worn pair of sandals. "See you at dinnertime, Pops."

She brushed past him, so close she could smell him—cedarwood and dirt. At least it was better than the smell of musty wood.

As she hopped down the spiral staircase, she dreaded that to grab her purse, she'd have to go through the kitchen where she knew Granny Em probably was.

Chloe took in a sharp breath as she pushed the swinging-door open. She could feel her chest burn as the scent of food in the oven reminded her of her mother's face of fury.

What is wrong with you?
Why can't you be normal?
Do you hate me? Is that it?
You hate me!

"Chloe!" Granny Em's lips curled so that the corners of her eyes wrinkled. "I was just about to grill up some sandwiches for our guests. Would you like to help me? It's really simple."

"No, thanks." Chloe reached for her purse. "I'm just headed to the beach."

"Okay, have fun."

Chloe slid out the back door and jogged down the cobblestone path. It was quiet on that side of the house, but once she got to the front where the guests sat on the wrap-around porch, she could hear their gossiping tongues and feel their eyes staring at her.

It was a small town. Everyone knew everyone. Even the travelers were often usuals who could date their vacationing to this very spot all the way back to when it first opened.

"Oh, look who's come for a visit. I had no idea," an old lady said, lifting her cane to point it at her. "You're the spitting image of your mother."

Chloe looked over her shoulder and nodded. "Thanks."

Before she could look back around, she slammed into a woman. Chloe fell backwards into the grass. The woman she had bumped into stayed standing, having caught the limb of a tree just in time. Chloe had never seen her before. She was about her mother's age, slender and pretty, with auburn curls pinned under a straw hat. She grimaced with red lips.

"You should pay more attention," she said.

"Maybe you should, too," Chloe countered, getting to her feet.

The woman huffed as Chloe raced past her, past the sign that read *Em's B&B*, and down the road toward the crystal-clear waters. At least there by the lake, she knew she'd find some peace.

Chapter Three

Emma emerged from the kitchen, her frizzy gray hair clinging to her cheekbones. She balanced a coffee pot and two plates of hot breakfast on a worn serving tray, the rich scent of butter and fresh bread trailing behind her.

Alexander and a man in a navy uniform sat around a table by an arched window that showcased the lake. The water was quite still this morning.

"Hello, gentlemen." She lowered the plates in front of them. "It's hot; be careful."

The man in uniform tugged at a shiny pendant on his vest. He smiled at Emma like Tim would with that twinkle in his eye. Emma pretended not to notice.

"If it weren't for your hair, I'd think you were only in your thirties," the man said.

Emma chuckled under her breath. "Maybe I am."

He gulped, then coughed, then looked sideways at the view outside.

"Emma, this is Captain Chad Monroe." Alexander lifted a flattened palm toward the gentleman. "He was my captain during my navy days. He's visiting from Vancouver."

"Nice to meet you."

"So, you own this place?" Captain Monroe took a hot bowl of oatmeal from the tray and placed it in front of himself. "It's quaint and makes me feel like I've stepped back in time," he said, looking around at the wood tables covered in striped yellow linen, all decorated with vases full of fresh flowers from Emma's garden.

"Yes, my husband and I have been running it since our early twenties. We owe the purchase to Alexander, here, and his lovely wife. We would never have been able to afford it otherwise."

"Alexander does have a habit of being generous." Captain Monroe slowly stirred sugar into his black coffee.

Alexander wiped his lips. "If I hadn't helped, you would've had to stay in my guest room and nobody wants that."

"No, too close for comfort," Monroe agreed.

As friendly as they seemed with each other, Emma could tell there was some tension brewing. The way they looked at each other, how Monroe would grip his mug a little too tight every time Alexander spoke—it was subtle, but obvious to Emma, who was used to spotting all the details. Things like that made her an excellent hostess.

The bell from the front desk dinged.

"I hope you enjoy your time here, Captain." She bowed slightly before scurrying off to see who was waiting.

A young man with blond hair slicked back behind his ears stood there, shoulders pulled back, foot tapping on the freshly mopped floor.

"Good morning, sir." Emma slid behind the desk and began checking her logbook. "Have you come for a room? We have a couple vacancies."

"Which room is my wife staying in? Her name is Julia Hedwink."

Emma rummaged through the guest book until she found the name. "I'll ring her room," she said, reaching for the phone.

"Just tell me the number."

"We don't do that here. It's a safety concern. Not that anything has ever gone wrong before, but you never know." She prayed the woman would answer to avoid added tension, but she didn't. Emma lowered the phone. "Sorry, no answer. Perhaps she's at the lake. You could wait in the lounge or grab something to eat. Since you're not officially a guest, you'll have to pay, but the prices are reasonable."

"Look." He leaned forward, elbows digging into the desk. His breath smelled of cigars. "I get it. You have to follow the rules, but it's a stupid one. She's my wife." He slid his driver's license across the table. It did bear the same last name. "I'm not some stalker."

"I'm sure you aren't, but I still can't break policy. I'm sorry." Emma spotted her husband helping an older guest down the stairs. As soon as the woman was on even ground, he strode over.

"Is there a problem?" Tim asked, standing protectively in front of his wife.

Mr. Hedwink pulled away, readjusting the collar of his striped polo. "No. I was just here to see my wife, but I guess it's not policy."

"No." Tim was quite tall and had a build that made him intimidating even in his old age.

"I'll just wait in the lounge." The man headed over to a yellow vintage sofa. Emma couldn't help but notice how empty-handed he was. No luggage.

"Did you check in a Julia Hedwink?" she whispered to her husband.

"I did. She was the one who arrived quite late—one a.m."

"Did she seem well?" Emma couldn't help but think of domestic abuse. It wasn't uncommon for a husband to arrive after his wife, but it was unusual for his wife not to be around when he arrived. It wasn't the olden days anymore. There were cellphones.

"I didn't notice anything out of sorts." He rubbed his wife's back. "I could call Henry. You know, off the books."

Henry was the police officer stationed nearby. He used to work in Toronto and had been quite busy there; here, nothing ever happened—something Henry complained of often. Still, it was better than being forced into retirement before he was ready.

"No, it's fine. I'm sure it's nothing."

But Emma knew it was something. This man had not come to the lake to relax and enjoy the scenes. He had come only for his wife.

"What are you doing?" Amber asked, coming up behind Emma, who was standing behind the front desk. "There's a bell for a reason."

Emma held up a hand, eyes fixed on the man across the lobby. "He's come for his wife," she whispered.

"And?"

"I'm waiting to see what happens."

Amber plopped into a spinning chair, crossing her legs. "You're not usually nosy." She followed Emma's gaze. "Though I must admit, he's easy on the eyes. You sure that's not the real reason you're staring?"

Emma rolled her eyes. "I just don't want anyone getting hurt. Something about him feels…off."

Amber grinned. "Do you mean to tell me Detective Ems is back?" She leaned back until her chair squeaked.

Emma groaned. "I just want to make sure his wife is safe."

"I'm sure he wouldn't do anything in the open."

"No, but one can get a good sense by mannerisms if there's trouble in paradise."

"And if there is, what can you do?"

Emma shrugged. She hadn't thought that far yet. "I'd think of something."

Amber began chewing on her necklace as she twisted in the chair. "You can't fix everyone's problems, you know. I get that's who you are, but it's not always possible."

"I know." Emma swallowed hard, thinking of her daughter. She was often successful at solving her guests' problems, but her own always seemed just out of reach.

The front door swung open. A woman with auburn hair walked in, wearing a long dress over her swimsuit, the scent of sunscreen clinging to her.

"Thanks for cheering me up," she said to the woman beside her. "Nothing like a good swim to clear your mind."

The woman smiled and pushed back her black hair. "What are friends for?"

Emma at least recognized the dark-haired woman. She was a local—Anne's daughter, Susan. It had been a while since Emma had seen her around and, though she lived just down the road, she usually kept to herself.

"Julia?" The man stood abruptly.

The auburn-haired woman flung her hand to her chest. "Kevin? How'd you find me?"

"How'd I find you?" The man towered over her. "I read the email your friend sent." He glared at Susan.

"You hacked into my email?"

"It was still open. I didn't need to hack into anything."

Emma's hand hovered over the phone, just in case she'd need to call Henry.

Julia's voice wavered. "Well, so what? You can't stop me from seeing an old college friend."

"Except you neglected to tell me you were leaving. One day you're next to me in bed, and the next you're gone. What are you hiding, Julia?"

"I'm not happy, Kevin." A tear slid down her cheek.

The man's expression softened, and he reached to touch her shoulder, but she turned away from him.

Kevin sighed. "I know." His voice was calmer now. "I get it. I've been gone a lot and you're lonely. It's just, sometimes I worry there's more than just a friend to visit for you here. Your email mentioned having dinner with a man."

Emma picked up the phone.

Amber grabbed her wrist. "It's just getting good."

Emma rolled her eyes and began dialing Henry's private cell. "Hello, Henry," she said when he answered. "You might need to make an incognito appearance at my place. There's an argument brewing between two guests and I fear it's going to get ugly real soon."

She hung up.

Julia gave a nervous laugh, twisting a strand of hair around her finger. "Really, Kevin. You trust me that little?"

He flung his hands in the air. "I don't know what else to think. You didn't tell me where you were going. I even made myself look like a fool when I tried to file a missing person's report."

Julia bit her lip and looked at her shoes. "I did have dinner with a man." Her body tensed and her cheeks went rosy. "He was a former boss of mine." She looked up at Kevin. "I just wanted to touch base, see if maybe he had some work for me that I could do over the summer. It was just a meeting between two professionals."

"So why are you blushing?" Kevin's hands clenched into fists. "Answer me!" he shouted.

Julia cowered, eyes sealed shut.

The room fell silent. Even the guests who had been minding their own business turned to watch. Julia's hands trembled. She looked around at all the people who were staring.

Tim stepped forward, his easygoing demeanor gone. "All right, let's cool it down. I think it's best if you take a walk, sir." He placed a hand on Kevin's shoulder.

Kevin yanked out of his grip. "I'm just talking to my wife," he said with gritted teeth.

"Look, you're scaring the old ladies." Tim glanced over at two old women who didn't look scared at all, more amused than anything. "Come along. Outside. It'll do you good to take a breather."

Kevin ignored him and grabbed Julia's arm. "Who is he?" His face hovered just inches from hers. "Tell me!"

Just then, Alexander strolled through the archway. "I left the bill on the table," he said to Emma. His gaze flickered to Kevin, then Julia, then to his wife. His posture stiffened. Without another word, he grabbed his coat and left.

There was something about the way he had looked at Julia that made Emma's heart sink. It couldn't be, could it? She looked at Amber, who hadn't seemed to notice.

Kevin's grip tightened on Julia. "I'm going to find out who he is," he growled, voice trembling with rage. "And when I do, I'll kill him."

The door flung open.

Henry stepped inside, uniform crisp, eyes scanning the room.

Kevin let go of Julia and stormed past the officer, shoving the door open so hard it banged against the wall.

Henry watched him go, then turned back to Emma. He pushed his thick-rimmed glasses up his nose. "Everyone okay?"

"For now." Emma glanced at Julia, hoping she'd say something. Anything. But, of course, she didn't.

Henry sighed. "Well, I'm just a phone call away." He walked over to Emma, folding his arms. "Coffee for my trouble?"

Emma smiled. "Of course."

Chapter Four

The nightstand vibrated.

Emma groaned, reaching for her phone—something she rarely used except to read the occasional book or search for a recipe.

She didn't even have time to mumble a groggy *hello* before Amber's panicked voice crackled through the speaker.

"He's missing." She sounded absolutely frazzled. "He's missing and there are police at the—at the shore."

"What?" Emma sat up.

"Alexander took his morning walk by the water, but he's always home by now like clockwork."

Emma rubbed her eyes, trying to push through the sleepiness. "Maybe he just got caught up talking to someone. Isn't his old navy friend visiting? Maybe they—"

"But there are police, Emma!" Amber nearly shouted. "You don't understand—he's never late. What if…"

"Amber, calm down. No one's called you, have they? It's probably just some homeless people setting up camp again or some teens making a bonfire. You know how it is."

"But I have a terrible feeling. I don't know why, but my guts feel all twisted up. Remember in middle school when my grandfather died, and I just knew? I just knew." A sob broke out. "Oh, my! What if…no, no…"

"Amber, Amber, calm down. It's going to be okay. I'm sure he's fine. Don't, don't cry." Emma slid out of bed. It was only a quarter to six and still dark outside.

"What is it?" Tim asked, rolling over to look at his wife, who was now by the window, looking out toward the lake.

"Amber," she said, putting her palm over the speaker. "Alexander's missing."

Tim sat up and looked at his digital alarm. "For how long? Ten minutes?"

"She's quite upset." Emma put the phone back to her ear. "Look, Amber, why don't I come by? We can go to the shore together and see what all the commotion is about."

Amber stopped her bawling. "O-okay."

"See you soon." Emma hung up.

"Do you think you can manage breakfast?" she asked Tim.

"Oh, gosh, breakfast? Really, Ems? You'll come back and the place will be burnt to a crisp."

"Just search recipes on your phone. It's not that hard." She grabbed her trench coat from the closet and threw it over her nightgown. "Amber needs me."

"All right. I'll try."

Emma hurried toward the door, but it hit something solid when she swung it open.

"Ow!"

She looked to see Chloe rubbing her shoulder.

"Chloe?" Emma frowned. "What are you doing out here?"

Chloe rubbed her shoulder. "The sirens woke me up and then I heard your phone ringing through the wall. I just, I want to know—what is it? Is someone in trouble?"

"Oh, you're a curious one." Emma buttoned her coat. "Look, it's probably nothing. I'm just going to check on Amber."

"Can I come? Please?"

Emma sighed and looked at the ceiling. "Fine, fine. I don't have time to protest."

As Emma drove Tim's big truck with Chloe in the passenger seat, she began to wonder if Amber was right about Alexander being dead. It seemed so impossible, and yet, she had been right about her grandfather all those years ago.

Chloe pressed her nose to the glass as they drove by the lake. It was swarming with police—some even from the surrounding towns, as evidenced by the names written across their cars.

Emma turned the corner, and the mansion came into view—a grand estate perched above the beach, its cream-colored brick walls glowing faintly in the early light. Large arched windows lined the façade, their interiors concealed by heavy curtains, keeping the world outside at bay.

In the center of the parking lot, a stone fountain stood like a silent sentinel, silver water cascading over the carved form of a boat's anchor.

This house had been in Alexander's family for generations, a symbol of old wealth and legacy. When younger, she and Amber would stare at it from the sandy dunes, spinning stories about what it must be like inside—grand staircases, glittering chandeliers, rooms so big they could get lost in them.

Chloe got out of the car first. "Whoa, this is crazy. Talk about rich. And right by the beach!" She looked over at the spiraling stone staircase that curved down the hill and stopped on the shore. "This would be a dream."

Emma approached the double doors, where Jared Pendlewood, the butler, stood solemnly, one hand resting over his chest. Age had carved deep lines into his face, making him a mirror of his father. His white hair, carefully combed back to disguise a growing bald spot, did little to soften the sharpness of his features. His deep-set eyes, dark and unwavering, held an intensity that made it hard to meet his gaze. A heavy gray mustache drooped over his thin lips, giving him a perpetually stern expression.

"Amber has been expecting you," he said, opening the door for them. "Right this way."

"How is she?" Emma asked, even though she'd know soon enough.

"Very unsettled. I was hardly awake when I heard the back door slam open and shut. She must've gone outside for a time, maybe to see if she could see him. She's right to worry. It's unlike Mr. Kirk to be late."

Emma could hear Amber wailing through the door frame. "Amber?" She knocked lightly on the old wood. "I'm here."

The knob turned slowly, and Amber peeked her head out. She dabbed her puffy eyes with her tissue, and stepped out into the hall. She looked over at Chloe, who was down the hall, poking a set of metal armor.

"You brought your granddaughter?" Her broken voice sounded annoyed.

"Don't worry. I'll make sure she stays in the car. I just figured I had to get to you as soon as possible and I didn't have time to argue with her. She insisted on coming."

Amber rubbed at her head. "I didn't want anyone but you to see me like this."

"Yes, I'm sorry. But let's go. No use wasting time. The sooner I prove to you the ruckus is over something entirely different; the sooner we can settle your nerves and they definitely need settling."

With her red, tear-stained face, Amber numbly followed her friend, without saying a word.

The beach was cordoned off with yellow tape, stretching like a barrier between them and whatever truth lay ahead. Police swarmed the shoreline, their dark uniforms stark against the pale sand.

Emma spotted Henry and waved him over.

Henry hesitated, looking from them to the scene, then sighed. "Mrs. Kirk," he said. "We've been trying to reach you."

Amber shook violently. "Wh-why?"

"Unfortunately, we have a body you need to identify for us." He took Amber by the arm. "Lean on me if you need."

Emma's heart sank. "I'm coming too."

Henry put up his palm. "No. This is a crime scene."

"A crime scene?" Emma pulled up her trench coat and stretched her legs over the tape. "Amber can't even think straight already. She needs me."

Henry sighed. "Fine, but keep your distance."

They didn't have to walk far. The body lay just inches from the water; the tide creeping toward stiffened fingers.

"Was it a heart attack?" Amber asked, gripping her handkerchief. "I knew he wasn't taking his meds like he should. I just knew it!"

Henry didn't answer. He didn't have to. As the crowd of police parted, they could see the blood speckled along the yellow sand. Emma lifted her phone to the top of her pocket and began filming.

Please, identify the body." Henry brought Amber close enough that she could just make out his face.

Amber sounded like she was choking. She grabbed her mouth and nodded. "It's him," she whispered, then she turned from the scene and vomited through parted fingers.

Emma rubbed her back and held the hair from Amber's face. "I'm so sorry." She pulled Amber to her chest. "I'm so sorry."

"I was right," Amber squawked. "I told you. I said it. I knew. But—but this. What is this?" Her body convulsed. "Was he killed? Did someone kill him?"

Emma looked over at the dead body. There was a gun in his clenched fist. "He has a gun," she whispered.

"Suicide," they could hear an officer say. "Typical for the elderly. Not much left to live for, I guess."

Amber looked over. She blew her nose in her handkerchief and walked over. Emma reached for her, but didn't dare hold her back. This was her husband.

"Alexander." Amber stood beside those who were taking pictures.

"Ma'am, you can't get too close," they said, holding up their arms.

"He's my husband. Don't tell me what I can and can't do." She pointed at the gun. "It's not his. That's not his gun. You said 'suicide,' but my husband would never commit suicide. Never! He-he was happy. He was. And that's not his gun."

"A Glock," an officer said, examining the gun with gloved fingers. "With a RCN insignia etched into it."

"Come on, Amber." Emma pulled her friend away. "Let's get you home. This will only give you nightmares."

"We're far past that," Amber choked. "We're in a nightmare already. Oh my, my Alex…"

Chloe was standing outside the vehicle, snapping pictures with her iPhone. She opened her mouth to speak, but stopped when she saw Amber's white face.

"Get back in the truck," Emma said. "I'm going to drop you off back home. I will be spending the rest of the day with Amber. Please try and help your pops. He can't manage the place all on his own."

Chloe didn't say anything, just stuffed her phone back in her pocket and hopped in the backseat.

Chapter Five

Chloe felt bad for Amber. Her husband was dead—probably murdered, not that that's what they were saying—the opposite, actually, but Chloe knew it was all too fishy to be just some suicide. And the way Granny Em was acting confirmed it.

'Amber said it wasn't his gun,' she had heard Granny Em say to Tim when they didn't think she was listening. 'And it is strange. Just a few days ago, we all heard that man threaten to kill him.'

'Are you implying Alexander was the man having an affair with a woman old enough to be his daughter?'

'Well, I don't know, but now he's dead.'

Murder on Lake Erie.

Chloe scrolled through her social media feed on her phone. She was worried that if it got out her mother would demand she come home. She didn't want to now; she wanted to figure this out because it didn't seem like anyone else with any amount of authority was going to. The headlines in the newspaper were talking suicide, but Chloe knew social media didn't play by the same rules. It didn't play by any rules at all. And sometimes it was far more truthful.

She searched for anything—rumors, theories, something to contradict the official story. But there was nothing. Just reposts of Alexander's eulogy and sentimental tributes from people who barely knew him—grocery store encounters, a friendly wave on his morning walks. Empty nostalgia.

Frustrated, she checked Amber's page. She had added Amber as a friend years ago, when Chloe was definitely not allowed on social media. Technically, she was allowed now, but only because her mom had installed safety features—and had full access to her accounts. Not that she ever checked. Too busy baking cakes to make sure her daughter wasn't chatting up a serial killer.

Amber's profile, once filled with pictures of her and Alexander at the B&B, had gone silent. No new posts. No replies to the condolences. Just an eerie, aching absence.

Guess she's in denial, Chloe thought. *Or maybe it hurts too much to remember.*

Chloe clicked on Alexander's profile next. She had friended him, too, back in the day. But it had even less than Amber's page, just some shared political posts and things about the Royal Canadian Navy.

Reliving his glory days, I guess.

She squinted at a picture he had posted of his business partners. Beside him stood a woman—the same woman Chloe had bumped into last week. Chloe zoomed in on her. Her hand was caressing

Alexander's forearm, and she wasn't looking at the camera—she was side-eyeing him.

Chloe remembered what Granny Em said and gagged. Why'd anyone like that want to be with an old fat guy? He was rich, sure, but still…

A knock at the door snapped her back to the moment. She slid her phone into her pocket and opened it.

"Yeah?"

Granny Em stood there in a long, black gown. Some blush was painted on her cheeks and she wore eyeliner under her eyes. Even Chloe found her pretty despite her wrinkles and obvious age. *I hope I look this good when I'm old.*

"The funeral is today. Would you like to come?"

"Won't Amber need you? I mean, I clearly was a third-wheel last time." Chloe didn't want to have to take the back seat again, even if it meant more time to investigate.

Granny Em shrugged. "Her children are home with her now. I don't think she needs me as much as she did."

"Well, okay. I guess I'll come."

"Do you have a black dress? I might have something that might fit you. It was one of mine when I was your age."

Chloe wasn't keen on wearing whatever ancient attire that would be, but she didn't really have a choice. She hadn't expected to attend a funeral while vacationing at the beach.

"I don't have anything, so I guess I'll wear what you have."

After the funeral Mass, everyone headed to the mansion. Chloe wandered inside, feeling like an outsider. Jared stood at the entrance; arms folded. Instead of properly greeting people, he just nodded as they entered. His body was rigid and his eyes glossy. He must've been close to his boss.

Chloe rubbed at the rough sleeves of her dress. It smelt like the drawers in her room—musty and old. Luckily, everyone was doused in heavy perfume or cologne, so she doubted anyone could smell her. And if they could, they'd probably think nothing of it. Their clothes probably smelled the same.

Granny Em touched her shoulder. "I'll be right back. I just need to talk to an old friend."

Granny Em waved at a woman in the corner. The woman was dressed in black, but had a red scarf around her neck, making her stand out like an apple in a basket of avocados. She stood with a glass of wine to her red lips, dark hair framing her pale face and showing off her well-defined cheekbones.

"Silvia! It's been so long!" Granny Em wrapped her wrinkled arms around her. "You look not a day over forty. How have you been?"

"I've been well. I'm just so shocked. To think Alexander's dead and by suicide! You remember our high school adventures?" Silvia smiled, raising her cheeks. She had a wistful look in her icy-blue eyes.

"He was always so confident, so sure of himself. He had a noble heart and always talked about joining the military, being a hero, saving lives. I would've never thought he'd take his own life."

Granny Em only nodded, though Chloe could tell she was holding back from telling her friend that she didn't think it was a suicide. "He was a good man. I'm going to miss him."

Silvia swirled her wine. "You still running your cozy B&B on the lake?"

"Yes."

"Solo still?"

"My husband helps."

Silvia gave her a knowing look. "I know you're the epitome of a strong and independent woman, but you're not as young as you look, Emma. Things happen in old age. Take the smallest tumble and you're bedridden for weeks. Don't ask me how I know."

"I know, but it's so hard to find reliable and affordable help these days, plus it's a small town. If I need to let someone go, it'll start a fire that'll never go out. I just don't want to risk stepping on anyone's toes."

"You can step on mine all you want." Silvia lifted her long dress to reveal simple sandals that didn't match her attire. "I'm staying with my daughter for a full month, maybe the whole summer—we'll see—and could help while I'm here. I'm sure Amber will need the support."

Chloe yawned into her elbow. So much for not ending up the third wheel. To be fair, she should've known better. It wasn't like Amber was her grandmother's only friend.

Chloe took a glass of fruit punch and a couple of chips and strode toward the end of the room. She looked out the window. A long wrap-around porch graced the back of the mansion, opening to a generous yard decorated with an array of flowers and a maze of hedges. Hardly anyone was outside.

She was about to turn back to the crowd behind her, but then she saw her—the woman in the picture, the one she had run into days earlier. She was at the edge of the yard, standing between two trees.

Chloe left her plate of chips on a nearby table and slipped through the backdoor. The hot air brushed across her cheeks as she approached the woman. She tried to be quiet and inconspicuous. The woman clearly didn't want any attention. If Chloe's assumptions about her were accurate, it was bold for her to be here.

A dark-haired woman pushed past Chloe, heading toward the auburn-haired stranger. She looked flushed and anxious.

Chloe stepped back and hid herself behind a small shed.

"What are you doing here? It's too risky!" The dark-haired woman shouted.

"I had to pay my respects, Susan." Chloe could see the line the tears made across the woman's blushed cheeks. "No one knows, but you and me, how I loved him."

Susan whipped around to look behind her. "Don't say that so loud," she hissed. "Last thing you want is for that little secret to get out."

"I almost want it to." Her voice quaked. "I am so tempted to stand on one of those tables and shout it out for everyone to hear. I loved him, and he—*he* loved me too."

Susan took her by the forearms and pushed her against a tree. "You need to go home. Kevin still loves you. He wouldn't have driven all this way if he didn't. And you loved him once. Maybe you could reignite that flame after you've healed."

"No. There is no salvaging that relationship. My heart has only ever belonged to Alexander. Kevin was just a distraction."

A warm breeze rustled up some old leaves by Chloe's feet.

"Alexander's gone now. He's gone. If he loved you, if he was going to leave his wife,—it doesn't matter anymore."

"But I can't move on. I can't leave. What if Kevin killed him?"

"You're talking crazy. Kevin's a hothead, but you and I both know he wouldn't do that. You don't even know if he figured it out. Did you admit it?"

"I didn't have to."

"Nevertheless, it's a moot point. Kevin still wouldn't have killed him. No one killed him. It was suicide."

"But why would Alexander kill himself? He said he wanted to come check on me that evening. He was worried I wasn't safe because of the scene Kevin made. If he was going to commit suicide, why make plans?"

Susan shrugged. "It may have been a spur-of-a-moment decision."

"It wasn't like him."

"That's what they all say." Susan took her by the arm and started dragging her further away. "Come on. It's best if no one sees you here. If you're right, and he was murdered—all the more reason for you to stay hidden. Kevin might not be the only one they'd point a finger at."

Chloe waited until they had retreated to the cliff's edge and then down the spiraling stairs to the shore. She slid her phone out of her pocket and opened the notes app. She jotted down the conversation the best she could remember. If she was going to solve this murder, every detail was important.

Now, to find her next suspect—Kevin.

Chapter Six

Emma scanned the large room; spotting faces she hadn't seen since high school. Alexander's son was by the punch bowl, and his daughter was by the windows, pulling the large drapes behind two armchairs to let the sun in, not that there was much sun. It was a gloomy day, typical for a funeral.

She brought a glass of wine to her lips, smiling at those who walked by. She had expected to find Amber with her children, but she didn't seem to be with anybody. Maybe she was having a mental breakdown somewhere.

Emma sighed and wandered down the hallway, peeking into rooms. Amber shouldn't be alone in such a state.

She pushed open the door to Alexander's former study. It was littered with paper and the drawers had been flung open. No one was around, but Emma couldn't ignore the sight.

"Hello?" She stepped inside, latching the door behind her.

The floorboards creaked as she walked across them to his desk. Her fingers hovered over wrinkled pages, stacked books, and his cellphone. It sat on the edge of his desk, touching a woman's trench coat draped messily over his chair. There were the first lines of a text message: "*I know you won't like it, but we need to discuss*"... And then fifty missed calls, mostly from Amber, but one from an unknown number.

She shouldn't take it. She knew that. The police should be the ones to confiscate such things. But they had dismissed the case, convinced it was suicide. Emma, however, wasn't convinced and while she also wasn't sure she wanted to get involved, she couldn't let possible evidence fall to the wayside. She gripped the phone and slid it into her pocket.

Who was the unknown caller? Why was Alexander's office in disarray? Whose red coat was hanging across his office chair? Emma sniffed it. Amber's perfume, which smelt of blossoms and vanilla, was embedded into all her clothes, but this coat smelt of coffee and sunscreen. Amber never wore sunscreen. She swore by a spoonful of cod liver oil a day, though it probably also helped that she wore a large-brimmed hat whenever she was outside.

The doorknob turned. Emma jumped and frantically looked for a place to hide, but that was silly. It would be far more awkward if someone found her under a desk than just standing here.

Susan appeared with her dark hair pinned into a bun. Her lips opened into a silent gasp when she saw Emma. "Oh, sorry." She went to close the door.

"What did you need?" Emma asked, no longer caring how things looked for her. It was far stranger for Susan to be here. Susan was not close to Alexander. Her mother hadn't been either. There was no reason for her to come in here unless… Emma glanced down at the coat. "Is this yours?"

Susan bit her lip, brown eyes darting from wall to wall. "No. I, uh. I was just looking for the restroom."

Emma forced a smile. "That'll be the door at the end, on your left."

"Right." Susan gave a brisk nod, closing the door behind her so fast she nearly snapped it onto her dress.

Emma touched the red coat. She almost wanted to hide it in case Amber saw. She didn't want her friend to suspect. Amber was already going through so much. Surely the last thing she needed was to find out her dead husband had had an affair.

But she didn't. She just left it there, hanging on the chair.

Emma did eventually find Amber sulking in the library. She was at the far-end of the room, curled up on the windowsill, looking at the lake folding in on itself.

"I don't know if I can live here anymore," Amber whispered, tightening her grip on her knees.

Emma stood behind her and placed her hand on her shoulder. "The memories might seem like a curse now, but soon you'll be grateful for them."

Amber shook her head and pulled a folded piece of paper from beneath her sweater. Her hands trembled as she held it out to Emma. "His will."

Emma unfolded the document, scanning the neatly typed lines. Amber and her children would inherit his assets and pension, divided equally among them. But the house—the sprawling estate that had been in his family for generations—had been left to the butler.

Emma's brow furrowed. "You see," Amber said, her voice hollow, "it's not even my home anymore."

Emma leaned against the wall, gripping the paper tighter. "That doesn't make sense. You should have a say in this. The house has always been passed down from the father to the eldest child—it should go to your son."

"You'd think." Amber shrugged. "I guess I shouldn't be too surprised. They were like brothers to each other."

"They seemed distant to me."

"Of course, in the public eye, that's how it should be. In private, though, they were close. Still, it makes me sad to think it won't go to our children. I mean, what will Jared do with his role reversed? I can't imagine."

"Surely you could fight it. It's your house, too."

Amber looked up at the vast ceiling, tears pooling in her grey eyes. "Like I said, I'm not sure I can live here anymore. Every square inch screams of him. I can't stand it."

"It doesn't come into effect until you're dead, though."

"No, it doesn't, but it feels weird to have my butler own the very roof that shelters me."

"I bet. Strange, too, that Alexander wouldn't have discussed it with you first. Are you sure it's authentic?" Emma traced the signature and the stamp of the notary at the bottom.

"Oh, believe me, this move has Alexander written all over it. He always left me in the dark."

Emma thought back to the red trench coat. *In more ways than one.*

Chapter Seven

Chloe lay on her bed with her elbows propping her up, and her phone on her pillow. She couldn't stop looking at the picture of the auburn-haired woman with her youthful skin and sparkling eyes.

A knock came at the door. "Coming," she groaned, sliding out from under the covers.

Granny Em stood in the hallway, her lips curled in a smile, showing off her cheeks that were dusted pink.

"Yeah?" Chloe leaned against the doorframe.

"I have a large breakfast to prepare for tomorrow. I was wondering if you wanted to help."

Chloe was about to say, 'No', but then thought better of it. If she was going to solve this mystery, she might need her grandmother's help. She knew everyone in town, and maybe she knew who Kevin was, too.

"All right." Chloe looked back at the phone on her pillow, then back to her grandmother. "I'll help."

The kitchen sat with its yellow cupboards and milk-washed counters. Chloe grabbed an apron from behind the door and pulled it over her head.

The dustings of leftover flour fell onto her tennis shoes.

"Here." Granny Em unlocked her phone and opened a webpage. *The Tastiest French Toast Casserole.* "Here's the recipe. I just halve the sugar. The amount of sugar they call for in these recipes is almost never needed and I'd rather not put any of my guests into a diabetic coma."

Chloe laughed a little, thinking of her mom's sugar-filled cakes. "Well, Mom didn't take that advice." Chloe ran her finger down the list of ingredients. "So one cup, then?"

"Yes, one cup, two pinches of cinnamon, twelve eggs, four cups of milk, a boatload of butter, and one loaf of my best sourdough."

"I thought butter gives you a heart attack."

"You believe that myth?" Granny Em snickered. "Your brain needs butter. It's what keeps it ticking."

Chloe shrugged. Granny Em didn't exactly strike her as a health-nut. "I mean, I like butter," she said, cutting the butter into tiny cubes and laying it out in the casserole dish.

"Rub some on the sides, too," Granny Em said, back turned as she set the oven to 415. "The better it's coated, the easier to clean."

Chloe touched the phone screen with buttered fingers, accidentally causing the photo app to pop up and reveal all her grandmother's latest pictures, including a video of the crime scene.

"Why do you have a video of the crime scene? Isn't that illegal?"

"Is it?" Granny Em shrugged and flipped it back to the recipe page.

"You don't buy the suicide, do you?" Chloe asked.

Her grandmother bit her lip. "I knew Alexander since grade-school," she said. "He wasn't the type. He joined the navy as soon as he graduated, always the hero. He wouldn't have left his family this way."

"I think it was murder, too." Chloe whisked the eggs and milk together.

Granny Em tore open the bag of sugar and began sprinkling it over the yellow liquid. "Murder's a strong word."

"It's the only explanation." Chloe leaned against the counter, fingertips dancing across the hard stone. "Can I help you solve it?"

Granny Em let out a breath of a laugh. "Your mother would murder me."

"Please." Chloe rolled her eyes. "She hasn't even checked up on me since I got here. Come on, Granny Em. I can help. And if you don't let me, I'll just do it, anyway. I've already gathered some useful information."

"We should leave it for the police."

Chloe eyed her grandmother's phone. "You don't believe that. If you did, you wouldn't have taken a video of the crime scene. Anyway, they aren't trying to solve anything. It's just us—doing their work for them."

Granny Em said nothing, bicep bulging as she finished the whisking.

"Mom said you were known as Detective Ems when you were younger, that people would come and ask you to solve their personal mysteries."

She sighed. "It was a joke. In school, I helped solve a petty burglary. Someone was stealing valuables from the gym lockers. It was easy to figure out."

"And after?"

Granny Em began slicing the loaf of sourdough. "Just simple mysteries—who liked who—nothing serious. And it's over now. I haven't had the time. I don't have the time."

"Alexander was your friend, though. The least you can do is find out who killed him."

Granny Em shoved the casserole into the oven so loud, it made Chloe jump. "We both need to mind our own business."

A knock came at the door. Granny Em pulled the oven mitts from her hands and strode over.

"Silvia," she said, opening it. "I wasn't expecting you."

"I figured you could use the help." Silvia smiled at Chloe. "Hello." She lifted a delicate, wrinkled hand and took Chloe's buttery fingers into her own. "You are the spitting image of your mother. My! It's been so long since I've seen her. I remember her when she was just knee-high. And now she's a mother! How time flies. I'll be in the ground before I know it."

"Oh, don't talk like that, Silvia. You and I both have many years left." Granny Em guided her to the counter. "I'm just preparing some breakfast items ahead of time. It helps to only have to reheat things in the morning."

"Smart thinking." Silvia slid off her wedding ring and placed it on a bookshelf nearby. "Where can I start?"

Chloe backed up. "Well, I'm going to go for a walk or something."

"We're going to have dinner soon," Granny Em said.

"Yeah, well, I'll stay on the property; let me know when it's ready. You have help now; you don't need me."

Chapter Eight

It was quiet on the lake. Footprints littered the shore, but its visitors had come and gone. There were only seagulls now, picking at the sand for food.

Emma sat on the beach towel beside Amber, watching the waves roll out from a sinking sun. Amber leaned her cheek on her hand. Fresh tears kept dripping off her chin, but she didn't seem fazed by them.

"You said he wouldn't commit suicide," Emma said slowly, contemplating with each word how much of a mistake it could be to say it out loud. "And that it wasn't his gun."

"Yeah." Amber took a deep breath. "But what do I know?" She shook her head. "There's no other explanation. Maybe he borrowed the gun or maybe it was his—a new purchase or something." Amber ran a shaky hand over her forehead. "I didn't realize I made him so miserable," she choked.

"Oh, Amber, no. You've been his light since senior year. No one else could get him to laugh like you could." Emma remembered it all like it was yesterday—Amber wearing her cheerleading uniform and blushing as the star quarterback escorted her home.

She had been poor, the child of a single mother barely making ends meet. It was the last thing anyone expected—certainly the last thing Alexander's parents wanted for him—to marry some girl who, to them, was nothing more than a pretty face.

But Alexander loved her. Even the long distance, when he joined the navy, couldn't stop them from being together.

"I was pretty then." Amber pulled her knees to her chest. "I'm just old and wrinkled now. And I think he'd agree. He certainly seemed to show me less affection. I can't remember the last time he made an effort to show me love…Maybe March?"

"It's easy to get swept up in our day to day and neglect romance. Many couples experience it."

Amber leaned till her shoulder touched Emma's. "You don't."

"But that's rare, and you know it." Emma couldn't help but remember the red trench coat on Alexander's chair. Had Amber seen it?

"I'm ready to go home." Amber stood and dusted the sand off her sundress. Her wide-brimmed hat momentarily hid the tears in her eyes as she turned to the road.

"Do you want me to drive?" Emma asked.

Amber dug the keys out of her purse. "Yeah, sure." The silver glistened under the soft rays of the lowering sun.

A gentle breeze hummed in Emma's ear as she followed her friend to the white Mercedes. The sand gave way to gravel, the stretch of yellow land to tiny shops and an open road.

A note fluttered under the windshield wiper. Emma yanked it free.

"Is it a parking ticket?" Amber asked, even though that made no sense. Their proof of purchase was clear as day on the dashboard.

Emma's breath hitched as she read the jagged letters, scrawled in red Sharpie.

IT'S ALL YOUR FAULT. I WILL MAKE YOU PAY.

"Uh, no, it's…"

Amber peered over her shoulder. "A prank?"

Emma forced a weak smile. "I guess." She crumpled the note, stuffing it deep into her purse, but her fingers trembled.

Amber sighed, pushing her hat down as the wind threatened to steal it. "Kids these days. Always up to something."

Emma nodded and got into the driver's seat. The car still smelled like Alexander's cologne. She swallowed a lump in her throat. She couldn't cry—not in front of Amber. It just felt wrong. He wasn't her husband, and even though they had hung out since high school, she never saw him as anything more than a friend that she wasn't that close to. She felt like she had no right to cry over him, certainly not with Amber watching.

"You want to stop somewhere first? Maybe grab a bite to eat?" Emma asked.

Amber shook her head. "I couldn't stomach it."

Emma couldn't remember what it was like to be that sad. She had felt it before,—when her parents died, but not in a long time. "You still need to eat.

I can't have my best friend withering away on me. Let me come in and cook for you. I could make you some borscht."

Borscht was Amber's favorite comfort food, and she never turned it down. It reminded her of her Ukrainian grandmother.

"Maybe tomorrow. I'll just have some cheese and crackers tonight. I think I simply need to sleep."

Emma turned the key in the ignition. "Are you sleeping?" That was another thing she remembered after her parents died—the insomnia.

"An hour here and there." Amber shrugged. "And mostly on the library sofa. Alex rarely frequented the library. It's the only place I'm not forced to remember him."

As Emma turned out of the parking lot, lights from a nearby car flickered on behind them.

Emma recognized the car—a shiny silver Kia. She had seen it parked in front of her bed and breakfast. She probably wouldn't have noticed it before, but the note left on the windshield heightened her awareness. Did the driver of that car leave it there for Amber to find?

She took a quick turn, and the Kia followed.

Emma swerved in the opposite direction and still the car was just behind her, its headlights reflecting in her rearview mirror.

Amber did a double take from her window. "You missed our turn."

"Someone's following us." Emma's voice was tight. "Get my phone. It's in the front pocket."

Amber unzipped Emma's purse pocket and handed her the phone.

Emma hit speed dial and connected the Bluetooth.

Tim picked up on the first ring. "What's up?"

"Someone's following us."

"Are you sure?"

"I've probably looped the neighborhood twice now and they're still trailing us. It's definitely not my imagination, and I'm particularly concerned because we came out to find a threatening note on the windshield just before leaving the beach."

"Okay, how far are you from the station?"

"Five minutes."

"All right. Head there. I'll get Henry to meet you out front. Don't leave the car till you see him."

"Got it."

"Love you, Ems. Be safe."

"Love you, always." There was a click as he disconnected.

Emma swerved onto a side street, weaving through the quiet roads. The car stuck with her. Her heartbeat pounded against her ribs.

But the moment she turned onto the police station's street, the headlights behind them dimmed. The Kia slowed.

Henry was at the front door when Emma pulled in. She looked in the rear view mirror, but the Kia was long gone.

Henry strode over to her window.

Emma got out of the car. "Sorry, Henry. I think they gave up the chase. The drama always seems to dissipate as soon as you show up."

Henry smirked, tapping at his badge. "It's the uniform." He peeked over her shoulder and waved at Amber. "Do you have the note?"

"I do." Emma pulled it out of her purse and tried ironing out the wrinkles with her palm. "Sorry. I thought it was just a prank."

He took it from her. "But not anymore?"

"The car was definitely following us. I even went in circles to make sure."

"They can't be too clever, then."

Or maybe just not from around here. Anyone else would've noticed that she was driving in circles, but perhaps not a tourist.

"Maybe it was a prank." He handed her the note back. "A coincidence? Who knows." He shrugged. "Nothing ever happens here, so I wouldn't lose sleep over it."

Nothing except murder.

"I'm worried about Amber," Emma whispered. "Can't you station someone to watch her house? I mean, this is a threat. What if Alexander's death wasn't an accident?"

Henry leaned back on his heels, wrinkling his mustache. "Look, I get it. You're a concerned friend. But that crime scene was analyzed by some of our best. There was nothing fishy about it. Amber's going to be just fine. And it isn't like she's alone. She has Jared, and he'd hear if someone broke in. His room is right by the entrance."

Emma looked from Amber to Henry. It all felt so off. That note felt like proof burning in the palm of her hand. Alexander was murdered. Maybe Amber was next. Emma didn't know what she'd do if she lost her. She had other friends, sure, but Amber was like the sister she never had. They were inseparable—total opposites, but two peas in a pod nonetheless.

"Henry, please." Emma's tone was like that of a pleading child. Her eyes gleamed as she looked up at him. "I know this doesn't seem serious, but I think it is. I really think something bad could happen. You wouldn't want that on your conscience, would you?"

"Look, I'd be laughed out of the station if I took a prank seriously. Nothing ever happens here. Nothing will." He rested a hand on her shoulder. "Go home to your husband and sleep it off."

Emma wanted to punch him square in the jaw, wanted to scream and make a scene. How could he not take this seriously? Wasn't it his job to keep the townspeople safe? If nothing ever happened here, then having a couple of cops do a night watch at her friend's house wouldn't hurt anyone.

"Have a good night, Henry." Her tone was sour, and she slammed the door as soon as she was back in her seat.

"What was that all about?" Amber asked.

Emma swiped at a stray grey hair falling into her face. "I asked if he could station someone to do a night watch at your house, just in case. He said no."

Amber leaned back against the leather seat. "I'll be alright. It was probably just a prank."

"Do you really believe that?" Emma turned to look behind her as she backed the car up. "I hate to say it, but I'm starting to think Alexander's death wasn't a suicide."

"Surely you're not suggesting..." Amber shook her head. "No, everyone loved Alex. He didn't have a single enemy."

"Maybe he did. Maybe you do, too." Emma held the steering wheel with a death grip. "I can't lose you, Amber. You're my best friend."

"And you're mine, but you can't seriously think this was a murder. Murders don't happen here."

"Being a small town doesn't mean bad people can't exist here, or visit." Emma grimaced at the towering mansion rising from the hill. "Do you want to sleep at my place?"

Amber shook her head with violence. "No. Alexander loved that place, and not just because his money helped pay for it. He loved your food, those cozy spots by the window overlooking the lake." Amber sniffled. "I'm better off sleeping in the library, like I said."

"But what if the person following us..."

"I can't live in fear, and you can't either." Amber looked at her sternly as if to say: *You are supposed to be the reasonable one. You're supposed to be strong and in control. Not me. Never me.*

Emma wanted to argue with that look, but instead she drove numbly up the driveway. "I can stay the night, if you want." A look of desperation, a plea. Amber wasn't having any of that.

"No. I will not have you neglect your business for me. I've already stolen a few days from you, and the reviews are starting to show it."

Emma raised her eyebrows at the comment. She hadn't even bothered looking at the recent reviews. "Fine. Just make sure you bolt the doors behind you and let Jared know about the threat."

"I will alert my watchdog, don't you worry." Amber leaned in to give Emma a half-hug. "Thank you for worrying about me, but I'll be fine. Prepare your breakfast, get some sleep, maybe bring me borscht for lunch tomorrow." Amber smiled as she pulled away.

"Lunch tomorrow. Yeah, sure."

Even after Amber got into the house, Emma stayed in the driveway, watching, waiting. She looked toward the stairwell that pivoted toward the shore, then behind and around. There was the fleeting sight of a rodent scurrying across the grass, but no silver Kia.

Her phone buzzed, and she picked it up.

"Everything okay?" Tim's voice crackled over the speaker.

"Everything's fine. I'll be home in ten; we can talk about it then."

"I'll wait for you on the porch."

"Thanks."

She hung up.

Emma rolled the windows down and did a U-turn. Her car rolled slowly down the sleek, newly paved driveway. The trees whistled as the wind blew across their barked skin. Toads hiccuped from a nearby pond. Mosquitoes buzzed; one flew into her car. Emma took one more look around before turning onto the street and heading home.

Chapter Nine

Chloe sat on the back steps just outside the kitchen entrance, the ends of her blue sundress tucked between her knees. Yellow tulips swayed between strands of grass. White orchards hung over a brown fence. Chloe's mother still talked about this enchanting garden. There used to be a small playhouse in the corner and a tire swing, but there was just a shed there now and a broken stump.

The back door swung open, and Granny Em took a seat beside her. "I'll let you help me, but no one can know, and you can't do anything drastic."

"You couldn't have stopped me, anyway."

"I know." Granny Em dusted off her apron, sending specks of sugar flying into the air. "Better I have you under my eye."

"What made you change your mind?"

"Amber's in danger. Yesterday, I found a threatening note on her windshield." Granny Em slid the crumpled note to Chloe. "Then I noticed someone following us in a silver Kia. We lost them when we turned into the police station."

"Yeah, that's not suspicious or anything."

"Cops won't take it seriously." Granny Em rubbed the wrinkles on her forehead. "You said you've been prying. Tell me what you've found."

"Well, at the funeral, I overheard two women talking. They mentioned a man, Kevin, and one of the women is convinced Alexander was murdered, too." Chloe took out her phone and opened a writing app. "I typed the conversation down as best as I could remember it. And I have some screenshots from his social media page."

Granny Em looked at Kevin's profile. Most of it was hidden due to his privacy settings, but she could at least see all the many pictures of him and his auburn-haired wife. He seemed genuinely smitten, but his wife's happiness was clearly faked, even in the wedding photos.

"She doesn't look very happy," Granny Em noted.

"Yeah, she's totally miserable." Chloe hit the screen's back button till she was at Alexander's profile. She scrolled down the page till she was at the business photo. "But not here."

Granny Em swallowed hard. "The coat she's wearing." Granny Em squinted at it. "I found that same coat in Alexander's home office. I can't believe it." She shook her head. "After so many seemingly happy years of marriage. Why would Alexander..." She looked toward the crystal blue sky. "Maybe it's not what it seems."

"Or maybe it's exactly what it seems," Chloe said. She looked toward the parking lot. Had she seen a silver Kia recently? Maybe. "I'll have to keep an eye out for the car."

"No." Granny Em touched her hand that was still gripping the phone. "Leave those things to me. You stick to the internet side of things. It's safer that way. If you see a silver Kia, call me, but don't get too close. Whoever is behind that wheel could be a murderer."

Chloe sat on the steps of the B&B, hearing the chitter-chatter of old ladies as they rocked in their rockers on the porch. She surveyed the parking lot in front of her, looking for a glint of silver, but there was no Kia to be seen.

She sighed, leaning back against the splintered steps. She wished she had been the third wheel that day. How exhilarating it would've been to be chased! And maybe she could've gotten a good view from the backseat and seen who was following them.

Her mother's voice played in her mind. *This isn't a game, Chloe. It's real life. You could get hurt.*

Chloe looked at her phone and scrolled through to see when her mother last called. It was weeks in the past now. Not a single phone call. Not a single text message. Nothing.

Chloe's throat swelled and her eyesight went blurry. She rubbed her eyes with the back of her arm. *It's whatever. She can hate me all she wants. It doesn't matter.*

But it did matter—excruciatingly so. Chloe slid into her messages and started one to her mom.

I'm sorry about that night. I didn't mean to ruin things for you. I love you.

But before sending it, she read it and reread it and then hit the back button until there was just a blinking line.

The sound of two women talking distracted her. She looked up to see Julia and her dark-haired friend. They stepped over Chloe and proceeded toward the parking lot, both carrying see-through tote bags full of towels, sunscreen, a couple books, and some of Granny Em's cookies in plastic bags.

"Thanks for coming, Susan," Julia said, readjusting her grip on the bag.

"The lake will help you forget him," Susan said. Her tone was indifferent, almost cruel. Chloe knew she wouldn't have appreciated someone saying that to her if someone she cared about died, but Julia didn't seem to register it.

Chloe waited until they were halfway through the parking lot before stuffing her phone into her back pocket and following from a distance.

The gravel caught itself under her toes as she walked after them. She groaned, yanking a sandal off and hopping on one foot while dumping the tiny rocks back onto the pavement. *Granny Em really needs to repave this*. She glanced back at the B&B and the shutters that were chipping paint. She knew Granny Em was busy either leaning over a hot stove or serving customers. She had no time to repaint the shutters, resand the porch steps, or repave an old parking lot. At least Chloe could help her with one task—solving who killed her benefactor.

"I still worry." Julia glanced behind her shoulder.

Chloe quickly slid behind a car. *Don't see me. Don't see me.*

Julia cleared her throat. "I worry his death wasn't an accident. We all heard what Kevin said."

Susan groaned. "Stop talking about it. The police have dropped the case. You should, too."

"They have? Like they're not looking into it at all anymore? How do you know?"

"My mom knows Henry pretty well. I had her ask about it like I told you I would. Leave it in the past, Julia." Susan swiped at her dark hair that the wind was blowing around.

Julia's shoulders seemed to relax. "I'll try." She glanced back again, but luckily Chloe was still well hidden.

Chloe took this as a sign she should keep more of a distance, so she waited till they were almost a blur before continuing to follow.

The sand was hot as coals, but Chloe was so tired of things getting caught in her sandals that she didn't care at this point. She took them in her left hand and trudged through the yellow specks barefoot, trying to keep to the shade so she was less likely to yelp.

Susan and Julia were at the shoreline now, dipping their toes in the water. Julia wrapped her arms around her knees and pulled them to her chest. Her auburn hair blew wildly, smacking at her face and back.

Chloe grabbed her phone, opened the camera mode, and zoomed in on them. She could see their lips moving but couldn't hear what they were saying. The crashing of the waves and the cawing of seagulls drowned it out from this distance.

She angled her phone so she could catch the title of the book Susan was holding. *Evil under the Sun*—an Agatha Christie novel. How ironic. And who would read such a book beside a mourning friend who had just lost her "lover" at the hand of a murderer?

Either Susan was clueless or her intentions were far more sinister…

Chapter Ten

The redolent kitchen smelled of vanilla and chocolate. Emma filled her piping bag with cream cheese frosting and screwed on a petal tip, decorating her chocolate-coconut loaf with curls of creamy white. When she finished, she sprinkled coconut flakes over the top. She took a step back to admire the nutty scent and the smooth layer of frosting that was perfectly distributed. She couldn't wait for her guests to try it. It was a recipe she hadn't served before.

She went over to the sink to wash the frosting off her fingers. Just before turning on the faucet, she heard Captain Monroe's voice filter through her open window.

"He got what was coming to him. It's done now. No use seeking revenge on a dead man."

Emma froze with her fingers on the handle. She peeked out to see his burly frame and him holding a phone to his ear. He was so close; she was glad his back was to her or else he'd surely see her gazing through the window at him.

"I know. I know you blame him. A part of me does too. It's why I came here. I hoped maybe he'd own up to it, at least. So many lives were lost that day. I know, I know. Samuel was the best friend and soldier one could ask for. I know." His shoulders were tense. His feet shuffled side to side. He couldn't seem to stay still. "But look, it's done. There's no justice to be had now. We can't prove it. We won't ever know."

He turned just then and looked in her direction. Emma quickly turned the knob and let the water hit hard against the metal frame of the sink. She kept her eyes on her hands, scrubbing at them as if there were blood on them instead of frosting.

When she looked back up, Chad Monroe was nowhere to be seen.

"Finish the cake?" Tim came up from behind her and kissed her cheek. "You're tense." He squeezed her shoulder. "Everything all right? Are you still worried about Amber?"

"Of course, I am. It was bad enough worrying that she'd do something reckless in her grief. Now I need to worry about someone else threatening her. I just, I don't know. It's all a mess and I miss my happy, funny friend. She's just not Amber right now." Emma sighed, wiping her hands on her apron.

"Healing takes time. She'll be herself again one day. You know. The wound is just very fresh right now—for all of us. You too." He let his hand rest on her rosy cheek. "I'm glad you're safe. Hopefully Henry's right and it was just a prank."

"It was a silver Kia. Keep an eye out." She lifted a finger.

"I will," Tim assured her.

She looked out the window. Where Chad had been was still an empty stretch of grass. "You checked in Chad Monroe, right?"

"I did."

"Do you recall for how long?"

"You'll have to check the books. I can't remember. Why?"

"I was just wondering. I was expecting him to leave after Alexander's funeral. I don't see why else he'd stick around."

Tim shrugged. "Maybe he just planned to stay awhile. There's a lot Lake Erie has to offer, as you know. It's beautiful in our little nook of the world."

"You're right. It is beautiful here." Her voice was soft.

His lips touched a stray curl on Emma's head. "You're beautiful. Let me take you out tonight by the water like old times; help you take your mind off things."

Emma blushed. "There's so much to do still. My guests will need more than just a loaf for their breakfast."

"Then do something easy in the morning, like scrambled eggs and bacon in the oven. We can't just let our lives run away from us because we're too busy thinking business."

Emma let her smiling lips graze his cheek. For a moment, she thought of Amber and the husband she had lost, and she felt guilty. Here, her best friend was without the love of her life, and Emma still had hers. She didn't feel she deserved it—deserved Tim. She was always so busy with things; always forgetting to take the time and appreciate the hunk of a man she married. "All right. Let me get ready then."

It was already past seven when Emma came down the steps, dressed in the same red dress she wore to prom decades ago. Her hair was pinned back, with ringlets cascading down her back. The sparkles on her dress glittered under the fluorescent lights.

Tim was waiting at the end of the steps by the double doors with his hands behind his back. He smiled wide when he saw her. "You look stunning."

Emma blushed, pulling a stray curl behind her ear. "It's so late. Everything's already closed around here besides the bar."

"That's all right. I wasn't planning on going anywhere." He pulled a basket out from behind his back. It was filled with a loaf of French bread, butter, jam, wine, and two glasses. "I was thinking we could enjoy the sunset on the beach."

Emma squeezed his bicep. "Always sweeping me off my feet."

He placed one hand on top of hers and guided her out the door and down the steps.

Emma looked back, catching sight of the empty desk before the doors closed. "What if someone comes needing a room?"

Tim nudged her to keep going. "Stop worrying. It's never busy on a Wednesday night and I left a note asking whoever shows to wait in the lobby, just in case."

"That won't result in a good review. Who knows how long we'll be?"

"A couple one star reviews increases credibility, don't you know?" He nudged her a little. "Stop worrying. Leave your people-pleasing nature behind and just enjoy our time together."

Emma sighed and rubbed her wrinkled forehead. "Alright. I'm sorry. I can't help it. I don't know how to relax anymore."

He chuckled. "You never did, my dear."

The sunset was a vibrant African orange, with the yellow sun hovering just above the grey-blue water. Emma dug her toes into the sand, which was still warm and comforting. Tim handed her a glass of wine, which she took between delicate fingers.

"To our life together. So many years, and I'm still far from bored." His cheekbones lifted as he clinked his glass against hers.

"Forever and ever, I love you," she said, bringing the rim to her lips and sipping. It was sharp, tart—stronger than her usual choice of drink. She had always preferred the sweeter alcoholic beverages—piña coladas and the like. But it was still nice to sip wine on the beach. It had been their tradition since University—not that Emma had gone; only Tim went. He chose to study engineering. In the end, though, he gave all that up to help Emma fulfill her dream of running a bed & breakfast.

"Do you remember how we'd all come down here as kids?" He leaned back on the towel, looking out to the setting sun that was now dipping its feet in the water. "Even the night of prom." He eyed her dress.

Emma smoothed out the fabric. She remembered it, all right. Riding in Alexander's Mercedes, Tim getting the door for her once they parked, how his fingers felt on her palm. The beach was busy that night. They weren't the only ones who had planned a night out by the water after the dance, but they had still managed to find a quiet stretch where they could set up their towels and watch the stars light up the inky sky. Alexander and Amber had sat just to the side of them. Amber had forgotten her sweater in the car, so Alexander draped his coat over her shoulders.

"I can't imagine being in Amber's shoes." She sucked in a shaky breath. "If I lost you, Tim. I can't bear to think of it..."

Tim pulled her against his warm chest. He stroked her back and kissed her hair. "I'm not going anywhere, Ems."

Emma sniffled, wiping her wet cheeks with the back of her hand. "There's no one as good for me as you. You're perfect."

"I'm not perfect," he said softly, a smile in his voice. "I'm just crazy about you."

She felt his lips curve against her temple, radiating warmth.

"And to think," she said, her tone lightening, "if it weren't for me solving the mystery of who was stealing from the lockers, we might've never gotten together."

"Why do you say that?" he asked, amused.

"Because it was my excuse to talk to you," she admitted with a sheepish grin. "I knew you weren't guilty—and didn't know anything about it—but Amber convinced me that if I had a reason, you wouldn't think I was, well…being forward."

He chuckled. "You accused me, though."

"No, I didn't!"

"You kinda did. You came right up to me, laid out all your evidence, and straight-up asked if I did it."

Emma's cheeks flushed as she giggled. "I was nervous, okay!"

"It's fine," he said. "It just meant I had to wait until you caught the actual thief before I could ask you out. I couldn't have you doubting my character our whole relationship."

Her laughter bubbled up, and she leaned her cheek against his shoulder, threading her fingers through his. "Well, I'm glad I found the thief, then."

"So am I," he murmured, pressing a kiss to the top of her head.

Chapter Eleven

Chloe sat across from Granny Em in what her grandmother called the guest parlor, the afternoon sun streaming through the window and turning their small booth into a sweltering oven. She wiped the sweat gathering at the back of her neck. *They really needed to upgrade the air conditioning in this place.*

The dining room was nearly empty, save for a man and woman at the far end, quietly sipping their coffees. Nearby, Tim moved between tables, clearing dirty dishes.

"Okay." Chloe took out her phone and opened her note-taking app. "What clues do we have so far? Who are our suspects?"

"Well, Captain Chad Monroe, for one. When I served him and Alexander, I could tell there was some tension between them. Then just a couple days ago, I overheard Chad on the phone with somebody, and he said that 'he got what was coming to him' and alluded to a mistake he made that killed a lot of people. I don't know if he was talking about Alexander for sure, but if not him, then who?"

Chloe typed Chad's name, 'suspicious phone call, a mistake resulting in people's deaths, maybe in the war overseas'.

"Then, I hate to say it, but Jared. I've known him for years and he seems harmless enough, but there are some things I don't think we can ignore. For one—motive. For whatever reason, Alexander left him the house in the event of his death. It doesn't come into effect until Amber dies or moves out, but it's strange he wouldn't leave that to his children."

Chloe's fingers contacted the keyboard again. 'Jared. Alexander's will; the house left to him. Is inheriting that mansion motive to kill?'

"Speaking of Jared…" Granny Em glanced around, likely checking that the few other patrons were still out of earshot. Lowering her voice, she continued, "When I arrived the morning of Alexander's death, I asked how Amber was doing. Jared said she was unsettled and that he heard her open and slam the door that morning. He assumed she had gone out to look for Alexander, but that didn't sit right with me, given the time she called. What if it wasn't Amber he heard? What if it was Alexander—or someone else entirely?"

Chloe pondered what her grandmother had just said. 'Heard door slam shut in the morning. Thought it was Amber.' She looked at Amber's name long and hard. Discreetly, so Granny Em couldn't see, she typed, 'Did Amber find out about the affair? Motive.'

"Then, there's Julia Hedwink. Based on the photo you found and the fact that what looked like her coat, which she was wearing in the photo, had been left on Alexander's office chair, it's likely she was the one he was having an affair with. I happened to overhear a conversation between two women just a few nights before his death. One, who I presume was Julia, was distraught because this man she claimed to love refused to leave his wife. Grief can do terrible things to a person. It's possible she could've lashed out at him in a moment of rage."

"We should add her friend, too," Chloe said. "Susan, right? I saw her at the beach reading Agatha Christie. Talk about ironic. And her dismissiveness toward Julia's suffering seems cruel to me. I don't know. Something about her character seems off."

"Go ahead and add her," Granny Em said. "And, finally, Kevin Hedwink. You weren't here, but there was some drama when he arrived looking for his wife. He argued with her and said if she was having an affair, he'd kill the man she was seeing. Can't get any more suspicious than that."

"No, you can't," Chloe agreed. "Anyone else?"

Granny Em shrugged. "Maybe his children. They always seemed cold to their father, and hardly seemed bothered at the funeral, but I could be reading too much into things. Not to mention, they weren't around at the time of his death."

"Maybe he just wasn't around enough for them to form a bond with," Chloe said, thinking of her own mother. While she did love her, it was hard for her not to feel and act cold toward a woman who barely made time for her.

"Yes. He was away a lot. We can leave them off the list." Granny Em retrieved Alexander's phone from her pocket; it was an expensive one—the newest and latest. "As for evidence, I have his phone and…" She rummaged through her purse and took out her own cell. "A recording of the crime scene. The footage is a bit rough, so I'm not sure what we'll be able to make out."

Chloe slid Alexander's phone toward herself. "I have a friend from school—total nerd. He should be able to help us with this."

"You sure you trust him?"

"Yeah. I trust him."

Chloe lay in her bed, staring at her phone, Mike's social page open on the screen. He wasn't really a friend. In fact, they'd exchanged only a few words all year—'It's okay' when he bumped into her in the hallway, and 'No, sorry' when he asked for her number.

What would he say if she reached out? Would she have to go on a date with him just to get his help? The thought made her shudder. She'd never live it down if anyone caught her on a date with Mike. It wasn't that he was unattractive; he might even be cute if he ditched the thick glasses and tamed his unruly brown hair. But he was painfully awkward, always rambling about conspiracy theories in class.

Still, Chloe couldn't deny she found his interests intriguing. If it weren't for her friends, she probably would delve into them with him. She had an image to uphold, though, friends to keep.. Popularity was important.

But now—now she needed the nerdy, unpopular guy.

Chloe clicked the call button on the social media app. She bit her lip, listening to the ringing on the other end. Maybe he wouldn't answer. Maybe…

"Hello?" Mike's face popped up. Like the typical male, he was holding the phone at a very unattractive angle that showed off his nose hairs and made him look like he had a double chin. "Chloe? Why are you calling? Is this a prank or a dare?"

"Uh, no." Chloe ran her spare hand through her hair. "This is going to sound crazy, but I'm visiting my grandmother at Lake Erie and some guy was murdered here."

"Ookay…"

"And the cops aren't taking it seriously. The murderer is still out there and may even be stalking my grandma. Anyway, I have the victim's phone and some footage of the crime scene. Problem is, the footage was shot with my grandma's low-tech phone, so it's practically worthless, and his phone," Chloe held the phone up so Mike could see, "Definitely locked."

Mike chuckled. "I didn't realize you were a real live teenage detective."

Chloe rolled her eyes. "Will you help me or not?"

She waited for him to say, 'In exchange for a date' or at least her number, but instead, he said, "Yeah, sure." No strings attached. Who did that?

"Thanks." She sat up.

"You got a computer?"

Chloe slid off the mattress and walked over to her desk. She slipped open her laptop and typed in the passcode. "Yeah."

"All right, I'm going to send over some programs you can use. This program will enhance your footage and zoom in on details that could help."

Chloe could hear him clicking away on the other end. "The phone is going to be trickier. But if we're lucky, the password will be something simple, like a birthday or something. Who's the guy?"

"Alexander Kirk."

Mike typed. "Former navy guy?"

"Yeah."

"Wife is Amber?"

"Yeah."

"Okay, got it."

More typing. "Try 062077."

Chloe tried, but the phone rejected it. "Didn't work."

"070278."

Chloe typed it in. "Nope. What are these numbers from? We only get so many tries, you know."

"Important dates. High school graduation, when he was fully enlisted in the navy." Mike rubbed his forehead. "Is he closer to his wife or his kids?"

Chloe shrugged. "Wife, I guess."

"Okay, try 080278."

Chloe typed it in and the dark screen dissolved to show a vintage picture of Amber when she was probably in her early twenties. She was wearing a white sundress and standing in the waves, looking back behind her shoulder, smiling. "It worked."

"Awesome." Mike turned to his door. "My mom's calling. I think supper's ready. Call me back if you need any help with the software I sent for the video."

"Yeah, I'll do that tomorrow." Chloe opened the call history of the phone. "I think this should keep me pretty busy for today."

Chapter Twelve

Silvia watched as Emma scrubbed at a raspberry stain on the mahogany wood table. Sunlight danced off the metal top of the saltshaker, momentarily blinding her.

"The fair has its grand opening tonight," Silvia said, taking the dirty plates.

Emma looked out the window. In the distance, she could see the fairgrounds. It was still too bright to clearly see the colorful lights. Right now, they were just faint glows of red, blue, and purple.

"Maybe Chloe would like to go," Silvia added. "I could watch the desk for you if you wanted."

"Are you sure?"

"Of course. I have zero responsibilities right now. My daughter doesn't exactly need me like she did when she was little."

"Are you sure you don't mind tending the desk? It's Friday night—bound to get busy."

"I think I can manage writing some names down in a notebook and handing over a set of keys." Silvia grinned. She leant forward and squeezed Emma's shoulder. "Go enjoy yourself with your granddaughter. You never allow yourself any fun. It's criminal."

"Okay, okay. I'll go ask her."

"Right now." Silvia took the wet rag from Emma. "Before you get distracted by something else needing doing."

Emma smiled. "Thanks Silvia. You're a good friend."

Emma knocked on Chloe's door.

"Who is it?" Chloe called back.

"Granny Em," Emma said. "Who else?"

Chloe unlatched the door. "Just making sure." She left it wide open. "Come on in. I have to show you what I found."

Emma closed the door behind her and pulled up a spare chair next to Chloe. "You unlocked it?"

"Yeah and check this out." Chloe opened the text message app and clicked on the last message.

'I know you won't like it', it read, *'but we need to discuss what happened on the last mission. I'm not the only one who can't come to terms with it. It cost lives, Alexander—a lot of them. But it's also in the past. I know that. Still, I think it would be good for us to talk about what happened.'*

"Chad Monroe," Emma whispered, her finger hovering over the name on the screen. "Was his number the missed calls?"

Chloe shrugged. "The calls from that morning were all from an unknown number, so who knows? But another message was sent just moments before this one." Chloe backed out of the message and then scrolled to the next one.

'I know you love me. All you have to do is leave her. Surely that would be better than living a lie—even for her.'

"This one is from an unknown sender, so it's fair to say whoever sent this message was probably also the caller. And we both know who probably sent this message."

"Julia." Emma took the phone and tried to scroll up, but that was the only message from this unknown number. Alexander must've deleted the others just in case Amber got ahold of his phone. "Why would he leave this message from her but delete the others?"

"Something must've distracted him."

"Or someone." Emma backed out and reread the message from Monroe. Maybe Alexander wasn't going on his morning walk. Maybe he was going to meet someone and maybe whoever that person was, killed him.

Chloe opened her computer. "My friend sent me some software so I can enhance the video you took. I can work on that now if you want."

Emma lowered the phone onto the desk. "No, that can wait. My friend, Silvia, has offered to mind the front desk, so we can go to the fair. What do you think? Sound like a plan?"

Chloe looked from her to the computer. "Honestly, I think solving this crime is way more interesting."

"Oh, come on." Emma playfully nudged her. "You need some fresh air, and so do I. It'll be fun. Plus, who knows what suspects might be around? Almost everyone shows up for the fair."

"All right, fine." Chloe pushed herself from the desk with her palms. "When do we leave?"

"Ten minutes. I'm old. Late nights aren't my thing anymore."

The air smelt like cotton candy and popcorn, buttery and sweet. Emma walked over to the food stand. Susan was behind it, an apron tied to her waist. Emma was surprised to see her. It wasn't like her to take such a job.

"Two pink cotton candies, please," Emma said, holding up two fingers.

Susan grabbed two paper sticks and spun them through the fluffy sugar. "Here you go," she said. "Eight-fifty, please."

Emma handed her a couple loonies and dollar bills. "Thank you. Have a nice night. Say 'hi' to your mother for me." Emma cringed at the forced line at the end. She really hoped she wouldn't. Last thing she wanted was to have her mother come by the B&B for a cup of tea and boring small talk.

Emma turned to hand Chloe the other stick of cotton candy. "It's the best."

"Thanks," Chloe said, chewing on the sticky pink threads. "I haven't had cotton candy since I was a kid."

"How has your mom been?" Emma asked. Her chest tightened, thinking of Bella. When was the last time she saw her? She couldn't even remember. "How's her business?"

"Uh, okay, I think. I don't know. Honestly, she's basically just a stranger living in the same house at this point." Chloe kicked loose some pebbles in the broken concrete path.

"So, she's a stranger to you, too? But you're her daughter."

"Only by blood," Chloe said. "I feel like I don't be—that I don't—that I'm not…I don't know." She shook her head, so her hair slapped her cheeks. "It's whatever."

"She loves you. When you were born, she called to tell me that she birthed the most beautiful little girl."

"Yeah, well, I couldn't cause much trouble as a baby. I just ruin her life now."

"Well, you are a teenager." Emma touched her shoulder gently. "I know she loves you, Chloe. You couldn't do anything to make her stop loving you. It's built into us mothers to love our children no matter what."

"I don't know. I think there are plenty of moms who are cut off from all that. And maybe she would love me if my mistakes were just your typical skipping school and sleeping in kind of mistakes, but I made a big mistake. It's why she sent me here."

Emma could see tears glitter in the corners of her granddaughter's blue eyes.

"She got a really good gig making a thousand cupcakes for some crazy fancy party—the biggest gig of the year. She had designed a massive cake for the centrepiece. It was super fancy and about half my height. But she was so wrapped up in this dumb event that she didn't even remember it was my birthday. I even gave her some hints, but it was like I was talking to empty space. All she could think about was this dumb party. I had enough. I wasn't thinking. I was just feeling everything—the anger, the pain, betrayal. I don't know, but I destroyed her cake. I went into the kitchen, picked up a wooden spoon and just went to town smashing it."

Emma swallowed. There had been a couple of birthdays she had forgotten as a mother. Running a business sometimes made the days all blend together. It was hard juggling the duties of mother and businesswoman. Almost impossible. One always seemed to go neglected—usually the most important one. "Do you want me to speak to her?"

Chloe shook her head violently. "No. I don't even know why I told you all this."

Emma grabbed her and pulled her to her chest, forgetting about the cotton candy and accidentally squishing it against Chloe's shirt. "You're a good kid, Chloe. I love you." She closed her eyes, trying and failing to remember how it felt to hug her daughter and when she last told her she loved her.

Too long.

Chloe broke the hug. "It's fine. Like I said, I don't know why I told you any of this." She scanned the field. The House of Mirrors sat just feet from them, screams of laughter resounding from inside its metal walls. Then there was the Ferris wheel, reaching toward the sunset, its lights glittering like starlight above them.

"Should we go on the Ferris wheel?" Emma asked.

"Yeah, okay." Chloe headed to the back of the line.

They stood there in silence next to each other. Emma picked at a loose thread on her sleeve. *Maybe I should call Bella when I get home. Or would that betray Chloe's trust?* She didn't know what to do, but she couldn't just not try to fix this mess, especially when she felt that it was ultimately her fault.

Chapter Thirteen

Emma handed Chloe a black tray holding two plates of scrambled eggs and bacon. "These are for Julia and Susan, table nine."

"Got it." Chloe tried not to lose her balance as she shoved her weight against the kitchen door.

She liked being a waitress until she had to transport the food—then she just spent the whole walk thinking of all the ways she could spill the meal all over the floor. What if some kid bumped into her? What if she slipped on something and crashed on her butt? It's not like she could see her feet with the tray in the way.

"Scrambled eggs and bacon," she announced, lowering the plates before the two women. She looked at each one closely. Julia was wearing the reddest shade of lipstick Chloe had ever seen, brown eyeliner, and a smudge of pink blush. Susan was bare-faced and looked tired, bags under her eyes.

"We're good now. Thanks," Susan said.

"Oh, right." Chloe jumped back. She had been so busy staring that she didn't realize she was still standing there like a total weirdo. "Uh, enjoy."

Chloe looked over at the other tables. Most had been deserted. Their breakfast hour was almost over, to be fair. But Chad Monroe still sat at the far end, sipping an almost-empty cup of coffee. He was looking at a newspaper that was last week's print.

"Hi, Captain." Chloe bent down and took his plate. "Finished?"

"Yes, thank you." He didn't look up from the page to make eye contact.

"How long will you be staying at the B&B?" Chloe asked, trying to make it sound casual instead of interrogating.

"Uh, another month, I guess. That's when my flight is scheduled."

"So, you just came to visit Alexander?"

"Yes. We were old friends."

"Good friends?" she asked. "When was the last time you saw him before…the…suicide?"

He lowered the paper and looked at her, a quizzical expression on his face. "What's with all the questions?"

Chloe bit her lip. "Sorry. Just trying to make conversation, you know. I'm bad at being social." She let out a nervous laugh.

"I see." He pulled the newspaper back up.

"Uhm, enjoy your meal," she said, hurrying back to the kitchen.

"Just Monroe and the two girls left," she said, as she walked over to Granny Em, who was busy with the dishes. "Uh, I think I might go to my room and work on that video."

"All right, dear. I'll stop by once I'm done here."

Chloe clicked the download button, then the icon that popped up on her desktop. When the application opened, she looked at all the symbols. There was a squiggly line, a camera, a magnifying glass, and a stop-and-go button.

She pulled down the menu bar and uploaded the video file. Once it appeared, she went through it slowly. She used the magnifying glass, but it only showed a blurrier mess.

"How do I enhance it?" she asked aloud, clicking random buttons to no avail.

She grabbed her phone, opened her social media and gave Mike a call. It didn't take him long to answer.

"Need some help?" he asked.

"Yes, please. I am absolutely lost. I have no idea how to improve the quality."

"Go to the control panel."

Chloe's cursor hovered over the panel.

"There will be an option called 'upscale'. You want to click that," Mike said.

Chloe clicked the upscale option. A clock symbol popped up over the video, and she watched the hand spin around the circle.

"It might take a while," Mike said. She could hear his chair squeak as he leaned back. "You gonna be there for the whole summer?"

Maybe my whole life if my mom doesn't forgive me. "Yeah, probably. Why?"

He shrugged. "Wanna go to a movie together when you get back?"

Chloe bit her cheek. "Uh, I don't know. Maybe." She felt bad saying 'no' considering how much he'd helped her, but what would her friends think? How would she navigate a friendship with the biggest nerd in school? It made her sick to her stomach just thinking about it.

He smiled. "No pressure. Figured I'd take the chance while I had your attention."

"What movie would you want to see?"

"We could make it Murder on the Shoreline. It's a murder mystery. Or maybe you'd want something fluffier?"

Chloe rolled her eyes. "You would choose that one, wouldn't you?"

"My choice would be the sci-fi dystopian Galactic Sky, but not sure you'd be up for that."

"I like dystopias."

"Even ones in space?"

"Yeah. I mean, technology is pretty advanced now. Maybe we'll inhabit Mars in this lifetime."

"Ha. Never thought I'd hear those words come out of your mouth."

Me neither. "Yeah, well, guess there's more to me than meets the eye."

"I know." A wistful smile spread across his face. "I could tell there was something different about you from day one. It's why I asked for your number that time. I guess I moved too soon."

Chloe felt heat spread across her cheeks. "Yeah, well, it was the first week of school and, I don't know, it felt like everyone was watching."

Mike laughed. "They were, but I get it. I wasn't trying to ask you on a date or anything. I just wanted to get to know you better." He leaned closer to his webcam. "So, tell me, what's your life story?"

Chloe laughed. "It's boring. My mom made the mistake of falling for my dad, who ended up being a total jerk. Left him when I was ten, or rather, he left us. Fueled by depression, my mom started up her baking business and totally lost herself in it. It's like the only thing she cares about."

"Yeah, that's their story, though. What is yours, Chloe?"

"Uh. I don't know. I'm just trying to figure out what I'm supposed to be doing, I guess. Right now, it's helping my grandma solve a murder. Not sure what it'll be after. What's your story?"

"I'm just your future famous hacker." Mike laughed, fingertips tapping a song on the wood of his desk. "I don't know. My family's broken, too. My dad's in jail."

"In jail?"

"Yeah, finances were tight. He tried to rob a store. It was dumb."

"Man, your story's worse than mine."

Mike grinned. "Every superhero's got a dark backstory. It's all about how we rise above our hardships." He tapped his cheek. "Anyway, I'll let you get back to solving that mystery of yours. Stay safe out there, Sherlock Holmes." He winked.

Chloe tried to think up a catchy nickname for him, but nothing came to mind. "See ya."

The call ended and Chloe shifted her attention back to the video. The image was much clearer now. She zoomed in on the sand at the many footprints, but she knew the answers wouldn't be there. At that point, with the police on site, there was too much traffic to make out whose prints mattered. So instead, she focused in on Alexander's dead body.

Seeing his lifeless eyes staring up at the sky made her shudder. *I'm going to have nightmares for a month.* She was about to skip to the next frame, but then she noticed something—a lipstick stain on his cheek redder than the blood on his face, a shade that matched what Julia wore that morning.

"No way." She screen-shot the image. It would've had to have been recent for it to look so bright. Would that have made Julia one of the last people to see him?

Chloe jotted that down in her note app on her phone. Then she went to the next clip that focused on the gun by his head. She zoomed in on the insignia. It was a sketching of four golden, incomplete triangles and an executive curl. She took out a piece of paper and re-drew it the best she could.

"All right, now to share this with Granny Em."

Chapter Fourteen

The humid, summer wind tangled itself in Chloe's blonde hair. She pushed the yellow strands behind her ears and started loading bags of groceries into the back of the truck.

Granny Em looked down the street toward the mansion on the hill. "We should make a pit stop to visit Amber." She glanced at her watch. "We have an hour to kill before we need to be back to cook dinner."

"Yeah, okay." Chloe hopped into the passenger seat.

Jared greeted them at the door. "Good afternoon, ladies." He stepped back and let them in.

"Hi, Jared. Amber in the library?" Granny Em asked, holding up a bag of beets, herbs, and potatoes. "I've come to cook some borscht."

"You won't believe it, but she's actually in the kitchen enjoying milk and cookies."

"I'm so glad she's eating something," she said. "Even if it is cookies."

She walked down the hallway toward the kitchen.

Chloe stayed behind on purpose. She'd rather be a loner than a third wheel. Jared watched her, looking at the high ceilings and the life-sized statues.

"Would you like a tour?" he asked.

"You mean it?" Chloe chirped. "That would be cool, thanks."

As they walked down the narrow hall, Jared pointed out the family photos. It was quick and precise: "That is Madame Sherri Kirk. She ran a small embroidery business that was almost as lucrative as her husband's banks. That is Sir Johnathan. Rumors have it that he left to become a missionary before eventually returning to the family business." But then he got to a black-and-white photo that gave him pause.

Chloe looked up at him and then at the photo.

"Sir Alexander Kirk." Jared cleared his throat.

"And who's the boy next to him? His brother?"

"No. It's me." He cleared his throat again and rubbed at his Adam's apple. "Doesn't belong here, really, but Alexander insisted. He always thought of me as family."

"Is that why he left you the house?"

"You know that?" Jared shook his head. "I can't say. I'll admit, that took me by surprise. He never mentioned his decision, and I don't know why he'd leave anything of importance to me. I'm just a butler."

"A butler who was like a brother. I don't know. Sometimes there's more than just blood when it comes to family, right?"

Jared lifted his shoulders slightly. "He was a good man."

"When was the last time you saw him?"

"The night before. He was up rather late. I woke up because I had heard a commotion down the hall coming from his study. I followed the noise to find him making a mess of his office, pulling out papers, looking for something, maybe. I don't know. It seemed rather odd. There was a gun on his desk, too. The one they found him with." Jared rubbed his forehead. His eyes went misty. "I wish I had taken it. I don't know. I didn't think anything of it at the time."

"Did he say anything to you?"

"No. I apologized and said I was only making sure there wasn't a robbery in progress. He thanked me for my service and bid me goodnight."

"Did you hear anything else that night?"

"I didn't keep tabs on the noise after."

"What about the morning? What did you hear?"

"The door slam shut. I assumed it was Amber. I'm not sure what time that was."

"Why did you think it was Amber?"

"Alexander never makes much noise when he leaves for his morning walk. Amber is the main culprit for slamming doors in this house, and she was frazzled that morning. I assumed she had gone out looking for him."

"You don't think it could've been someone else?"

"No. Alexander didn't have any guests over that night." He studied Chloe's face. "Trying to piece it all together, are you?"

Chloe shrugged. "Yeah, well, how someone died is in some ways far more interesting than how they lived."

The garden in front of the wrap-around porch was Emma's favorite part about the property. Even in the winter, when the flowers withered up, the large cypress trees that towered overhead would hang like beautiful green garlands, stretching toward the grass and the cobblestone path.

Emma smiled, remembering how Bella would color the stones with chalk. Those images were long gone now, washed away by a thousand rainfalls. But Emma could still see them, could still hear her daughter's voice asking if she could just join her for one second. Emma tried to think of a time she said 'yes'. If she ever had, she couldn't remember. Usually, she said she was too busy, and once she even scolded her because—what would the guests think of a child's drawings littering the pathway?

A light shining from above the gabled roof, stretching across the path, distracted Emma from her thoughts. Emma looked up to see her granddaughter's thin silhouette behind the curtains. Emma couldn't go back in time. She knew that. Now was the time to go forward.

She had to stop Bella from making her mistakes. No business was more important than family. Maybe it was too late for Emma to make up for her absence, but it wasn't for Bella.

Emma took her cell out of her apron pocket and dialed Bella's number.

"What's wrong?" Bella asked. "Chloe do something?"

Emma paused, trying to think up what she was going to say. "Chloe's fine. She hasn't done anything troublesome. But I need to talk to you, Bella. I think—I know I made a lot of mistakes raising you. I was absent a lot, distracted. I didn't spend time with you like I should have, and I'm so sorry."

Bella groaned. "Mom, seriously, it's fine. I'm fine. Don't worry about it."

"I think you're making the same mistakes. Chloe is more important than a cake."

"Of course, she's more important than a cake," Bella barked. "Who said she wasn't? What are you insinuating? Are you insinuating I'm a bad mother? What would you know? You're not around."

"Chloe told me that you two had a fight and—"

"Yeah, so what? People argue. It's a normal part of life."

"And you haven't called her."

Chloe doesn't want me bothering her with a phone call. She hates when I call. And, seriously, I work such long hours just to keep a roof over our heads and to make sure she has everything she needs."

Emma sighed. "Bella, I'm not trying to criticize you. I know you love your daughter and you're trying so hard to give her a wonderful life. I just think you might need to show her in a way she can understand."

"Yeah, okay." Bella huffed. "I'll call her. Happy?"

Emma inhaled sharply. "I love you," she whispered just before the line went dead.

Chapter Fifteen

Chloe sat where the water kissed the sand, not caring about her now-soaked dress, just relishing in the cool brush of waves lapping at her ankles.

She held her phone in her hand. There had been several missed calls from her mother. Chloe sighed and hit the dial button beside her mother's picture.

It hardly rang.

"Hello?" Mom's voice sounded irritated. "Chloe?"

"Hi, mom. I saw you called. What's up?"

"I just wanted to check in. How are things? Ready to come home? I know there's not much to do in a small town like that. I just wanted to let you know that if you want to come home early, the door's open."

"Uh, thanks, but I'd rather stay till the end of summer, like we planned. I'm actually liking it here."

"Oh." She sounded surprised. "Well, that's good to hear."

Chloe could hear her mother's earrings tapping against the phone.

"How are you?" Chloe asked. Really, she just wanted to hang up. Every single word she spoke felt forced.

"Doing well. I managed to remake that cake with some help from Gretchen who runs the bakery next door, so the event went better than I thought it would and it looks like I'll have a repeat customer, so everything's going well over here. I'm, uh, I'm sorry for losing my cool and forgetting what day it was."

"It's okay. I'm sorry, too."

"You still don't want to come home?"

"Not yet."

"Okay, well, let me know if you change your mind. I have to go now. I have a dozen cookies to bake for tomorrow. You know how it is. I'm sure your Granny Em is keeping you busy in the kitchen."

"Yeah, sometimes, but it's way chillier in her kitchen than…" Chloe bit her lip before finishing. "Anyway, I'll let you go."

Mom sighed. "All right, bye, Chloe. Love you."

"Love you, too," Chloe forced out before hitting the red hang-up button.

Chloe got to her feet, yanking at her dress that was sticking to her wet thighs. In the direction of the B&B, she could see Julia strolling down the sidewalk. Chad Monroe was walking beside her, and she was laughing at something he had said.

What on earth? Chloe held her phone in their direction and snapped a photo. *So, Julia knows Chad now? Since when?*

Chloe walked toward them, her phone in her hand. As she passed, she could hear Chad say, "I had no idea you used to work with Alex. It's not like him to hire a pretty thing as his secretary. He usually always hired grandmas."

Julia paused, her eyes making contact with Chloe. "I had just the skill set he needed, I guess." Julia shrugged, turning from Chloe to Chad again. "So strange to think he's dead now."

"Strange, indeed."

Chloe tried to slow her pace to hear more, but she didn't want to draw their attention anymore than she already had. So, instead of continuing to follow, she let them disappear down the sidewalk.

Chapter Sixteen

Emma walked out to the front of her B&B, lugging a garbage bag from her kitchen. It was then she noticed it—a silver Kia parked along the sidewalk. She threw the stinky garbage into the dumpster, dusted off her hands, and walked toward the car for a closer look.

Through the passenger window, she could make out a man's profile.

Emma got into her husband's truck and waited. Who was it and what was he doing here? Where was he planning to go after? Her metal bracelet clanged against the leather steering wheel.

It felt like forever before the Kia finally pulled out and started driving down the road. Emma discreetly followed.

Little shops painted in various hues of blue, yellow, and pastel pink passed her by in a blur as she drove. She watched as the car pulled into the parking lot of Sunshine Motel, Emma's fiercest competitor. *Low Prices Always*, the blinking sign read.

Emma parked along the road and got out. The Kia stayed running for a while. As she got closer, she could hear rock music through the windows.

Finally, the door opened, and Kevin got out, dressed in a fancy suit that made him look very out of place.

Emma's fingers tightened into fists. Deep in her gut, she knew it had to be him. He had to be the murderer. But why was he threatening Amber? That part didn't make sense. Amber had suffered the same cruelty he had, having been cheated on.

Kevin walked over to a pastel blue door and took his key from his back pocket. He dropped it on the pavement, bent over to pick it back up, and inserted it into the lock.

Room 67.

Emma took out her phone and snapped pictures of the silver Kia and of Kevin just before he disappeared behind the closed door. Then she texted Chloe: *'Check this out. Scour the internet. See what dirt you can find. I think we have our killer.'* And attached the photos to the message.

Emma sat on the end of her bed with her legs curled under her. Amber had always marveled at her retained flexibility. "I found the murderer."

Tim was buttoning up his pajama shirt, his movements slow and methodical.

"The driver of the silver Kia is Kevin. I saw him outside our B&B and followed him to see where he'd go."

Tim stopped mid-button and looked up. "You plan to take it to Henry?"

Emma shook her head. "You know he won't take it seriously. I need more evidence before I go to him."

Tim sighed heavily, the mattress dipping under his weight as he sat down beside her. "This is serious, Ems. If you're going to accuse someone of murder, you need to be sure."

"And I will be."

Tim rubbed the wrinkles on his forehead. "And be careful. You shouldn't have followed him. What if he had seen you?"

"He didn't. I was careful, I promise."

Tim arched an eyebrow, unconvinced. "You're not exactly a trained spy, Ems. I have my doubts you were as hidden as you thought."

"He didn't even glance in my direction."

"That you saw." Tim reached over, gently taking her hand. His voice softened. "I know fixing things is your passion, but this might be beyond your expertise. This isn't a simple case of a locker-burglar. This is murder. You could get hurt."

"No one's paid me any mind so far." Emma squeezed his hand, her gaze steady. "Stop worrying. I'm perfectly safe." She leaned in and pressed a soft kiss to his lips. "Promise."

Chapter Seventeen

Chloe sat on her windowsill, looking out toward the lake with her phone on her lap. She had asked Mike to run a search on Kevin, but it had proven unsuccessful so far. He had no criminal record or sad backstory, and his social media presence was insignificant—just some pictures of his wedding and work-related stuff. He didn't even share political posts.

She looked at Alexander's phone on the table nearby and grabbed it. *Maybe I missed something.*

Chloe started scrolling through the messages and call history. Mike had found Kevin's number. Maybe if she searched for it in Alexander's phone's log…

"There it is," she said aloud, her palm over her lips. Kevin had called Alexander the day before he was murdered.

This didn't prove murder, but it did signify Kevin may have been able to identify the man his wife was cheating on him with, the man he had sworn to kill.

I have to tell Granny Em! Chloe slid off the ledge, rushed through her doorway, down the hall and wooden stairwell, turned through the dining room, and entered the kitchen.

"I found his number in Alexander's phone log!"

Granny Em spun around. Her hands were dusted in flour, as were her rosy cheeks. "Whose number? Kevin's?"

"Yes. My friend was able to find it; I plugged it into the log history, and sure enough, it popped up." Chloe held up the phone so her grandmother could see. "That's his number, and the call was made the day before his death."

Granny Em leaned back against the counter. "So, Kevin found out the identity of the man he had sworn to kill."

"Are we going to take it to the police?"

Granny Em shook her head. "I don't know if it's enough, sadly. I mean, he threatened to kill Alexander in front of quite a crowd, and that wasn't even enough. We need something else—something more."

Chloe's phone vibrated. She slid it out of her pocket and read a message from Mike.

'Found something. Apparently, there was a ship that sank during a storm. Your victim was on that ship. He was second-in-command. Guess who else was on that ship. Kevin's twin brother. I've attached the article.'

Chloe opened the attachment. The article talked about how the ship was designed to rough such a storm and that there were complaints from surviving lower officers that the higher-ups ignored reported safety concerns. Kevin, in an interview, was recorded as saying, "The commanding officers were responsible for my brother's death. If it's the last thing I do, I will ensure justice is served." Chloe scanned through the names of the dead as well as the survivors. Second-in-command Alexander Kirk was named as one of the higher-ups.

"Look at this." Chloe held her phone up to Granny Em. "Looks like there could've been even more motive than we originally suspected."

Granny Em took the phone from her, nodding slowly. "Motive indeed."

Chapter Eighteen

Emma woke to her phone vibrating on her nightstand. In her groggy state, she grabbed it and put it to her ear.

"Someone just tried to break into my house." Amber's voice shook as she spoke.

"What?" Emma flung forward much too fast—her head was spinning as a result. "Are you okay?"

"I'm fine. The police are on their way, and whoever it was is gone now. They didn't get inside, I don't think. After that incident with the car following us, I installed some sensors for the evening and early morning hours. At about four a.m., they went off, which triggered the alarm. I think that noise must've scared whoever it was. I called the police as soon as I heard it."

"Did you see anything out the window?"

"No, the morning fog was too thick." Amber sighed. Emma could hear the sleeve of her shirt brushing against the phone.

"Do you want me to come over?"

"I think I'll be okay. I just wanted to talk to somebody. Maybe the security camera picked something up. I guess I'll have to get Jared to send the cops the footage."

"Security camera? I remember you and Alexander talking about that, but didn't realize you installed any."

"Oh, yeah, we installed them last year."

"Last year?" Emma rubbed at her wrist. "Could I look at the footage before you send it over? I can come now."

"Uhm, I guess."

"Great. See you soon."

By the time Emma arrived, the police were already there talking with Amber on the porch steps. Emma rushed over. She needed to see that footage before they confiscated it.

"Everything all right?" she asked, touching Amber's shoulder. "Can I see the footage?" she mouthed, her back to the officers so they couldn't read her lips.

"Jared's in the office," Amber said, rubbing the goosebumps on her arms.

Emma nodded. "We can have tea once the police finish up. It should help calm your nerves," she said, before heading inside.

Alexander's office looked cleaner than it had the day of the funeral. The papers that were in disarray were now neatly organized in piles on his desk, and the red coat that had hung on his chair was gone. Emma wondered if Susan had successfully retrieved it once Emma had left, or if Amber had been the one to find it. If Amber had—what did she think? Did she just assume someone had left it there from the funeral, or did she suspect an affair?

"Amber said you wanted to see the footage?" Jared pushed back on the wheels of the chair.

The video quality was grainy and hard to see, but the car certainly matched the description of Kevin's silver Kia. Emma watched the vehicle pull up to the front door and a figure in a trench coat got out. It was just a quick blur of an image. The shrubbery hid the person too well to have any hope of identifying them.

"Can you show me the footage for the day Alexander was found dead?"

Jared looked up at Emma, his bushy eyebrows creasing. "Why? What are you thinking?"

"I'd just like to see it."

Jared typed in the dates and pulled up the footage. Emma leaned toward the screen. 4:40 a.m., twenty minutes before Alexander would head out for his walk. Jared tapped his fingers to the desk.

Then it appeared—the same light-coloured car. "It's the same." Emma's finger smeared the screen. "Is there a license plate?"

Jared shook his head. "No, whoever is driving seems to know exactly where the cameras are because they always pull in their car in such a way, we can't see that or their face." He rubbed at his chest and cleared his throat. "Do you think he was murdered?"

"Well, murdered or not, whoever tried to break in this morning was the same person who visited Alexander the morning of his death." Emma pulled back and took her phone out of her purse. She looked again at the photos of Kevin exiting his car. She showed them to Jared. "This looks like the same car, right?"

Jared nodded. "But why would someone murder Alexander, and if they did, why would they be so bold as to try and break in after his death?"

Emma tapped her chin. "Maybe there's evidence here that was left behind. Did you clean Alexander's office, or was that Amber?"

"It was me. Amber still avoids the rooms he frequented."

"Did you find anything?"

"A coat I didn't recognize." He shrugged. "That's about it. The only odd thing was the mess. Alexander usually kept things neat, but he must've lost something because the day before, I found him rummaging through his drawers. Not sure what he would have been looking for. I'm just surprised he would have left it in such a state. He was usually quite meticulous about where things were placed."

"Right." *Chloe mentioned that.* "Hmm, I wonder what he was looking for." Emma looked at the screen and the shadowy figure that was mostly obscured by the bushes. "Maybe they are looking for it, too."

Just then, Henry came through the door. "I've come for the security footage." He scrutinized

Emma as he got closer, asking with his eyes what on earth she was up to, but he didn't say anything.

"All here." Jared stood and pointed to the chair. "It was hard to make out who it was. They seemed to know ahead of time where all the blind spots were."

"So, whoever it was must know Alexander on a personal level," Emma said. "At least well enough to know the layout of his house."

Henry shrugged. "Thieves have an eye for things. With the right equipment, you can easily spot a security camera ahead of time."

"The car that showed up this morning also showed up the morning of Alexander's murder—I mean death." Emma bit the bottom of her lip. "They entered the house that time, though, and didn't seem to experience any trouble getting in."

Henry raised a brow at her. "Right. Well, maybe it is someone he knew. Does Amber recognize the vehicle?"

"She hasn't seen the footage yet," Jared said. "Too spooked. Her nerves aren't quite the same since he was found."

"Well, ask her if she recognizes it. Maybe it was just a friend visiting."

"At four a.m.?" Emma's jaw dropped. The dismissiveness was mind-boggling to her. "And if it was just a friend, why leave when the alarms went off?"

Henry looked sideways at her. "Do you have any ideas, Sherlock Holmes?"

"The car in the footage looks very similar to a car belonging to a Kevin Hedwink. He was the one who may have threatened Alexander, too."

"Oh?"

"His wife was having an affair with who I believe was Alexander, and Kevin said if he found out who he was, he'd kill him. This was just days before the mur—he was found dead."

"Why do you think Alexander was having an affair? He seemed happily married to me."

Emma looked to the hallway. There was no sign of Amber, but that didn't mean she wasn't close enough to hear. Still, this was a matter of life or death and eventually she was bound to find out, anyway. "Uhm, he did seem to be happily married, but there were signs. Some pictures on his social media link him to Julia Hedwink. I found a coat in his office that matched the one she was wearing in that picture. There have been some conversations I've overheard that would suggest the affair, as well. Of course, I'm not certain."

"Of course." Henry grimaced. "Well, I'll consider seeking out this Kevin Hedwink and asking him some questions, but technically there was no break-in. The door doesn't even seem to be tampered with, so even if he was the one who showed up this morning, we may not be able to charge him with a crime."

Not this one, maybe.

Chapter Nineteen

Emma sat parked outside the door with the bold, black 67 over it. The silver Kia wasn't here, neither were the cops. And she knew they wouldn't come. She could tell by Henry's mannerisms that he wasn't going to bother following up. It made her blood boil. She gripped the steering wheel so tight her knuckles turned white. What would've happened if Kevin had broken in? Was he looking to take something, or was he planning to kill Amber next? The only car around when that threatening note was found had been his.

It didn't make sense why he'd want to kill Amber. What had she done? Still, Emma knew that sometimes the motive didn't need to make sense. All the signs pointed to Kevin and she was the only one who could prove it.

Emma got out of the car and walked to the door. She looked through the window. The place was near-empty. She could see a cup of water on his nightstand, but that was it. She looked at the door handle. She could maybe search online for a break-in tutorial, but that felt terribly wrong even given the circumstances.

"Stalking me?" The voice was sleek and smooth, like the voice of a serpent. She could smell cigarette smoke reeking from his clothes as she spun around.

Emma swallowed the saliva that seemed to suddenly stick to her throat like toothpaste.

"I just wanted to ask you something." It was a lie. She had not intended to come into contact with the murderer himself, not even to interrogate him.

"Okay." He bit his cheek. His blue eyes looked her over.

Emma imagined those icy eyes looking down at Alexander's lifeless body and her blood began to boil again. She rummaged through her purse and saw Alexander's phone, but before withdrawing it, she texted Henry as discreetly as she could manage.

I may need help. Room 67 at Sunshine Inn.

Then she hit the record button.

"I found this." She took out Alexander's phone. "You called Alexander Kirk." She flashed the screen in his face, revealing his number. "That's your number, right?"

"Uh, yes. What's your point?"

"You were one of the last people to call him and now he's dead. Your car was also seen at four a.m. pulling up his driveway this morning. Why?"

"I was still sleeping at four a.m. I certainly didn't drive to the Kirk residence."

"Your car was caught on camera."

"It wasn't my car."

"And I guess you'd say it also wasn't your car that stalked me and Amber? It wasn't you that left that note on her windshield?"

"You're a crazy old bat!" He laughed, ruffling his blond hair with sweaty fingers. "No, I didn't leave any notes or stalk anybody. I don't know what kind of game you're playing, but you're wasting your time and mine." He tried to get past her to the door. "If you'll excuse me, I need to get to my room."

Emma positioned herself so she was completely blocking the entrance. "Look, I don't know if you killed him because of what happened with your brother or your wife, but Amber is innocent. If you think she isn't, you're wrong. I've known her all my life. Whatever mistake Alexander made when he was second-in-command, Amber would've had zero say in it."

Kevin flinched. "My brother? What do you know of my brother? And why would I care about Alexander's wife?" He shook his head. "Just get out of my way. I know you oldies like to tell stories, but I don't have time for this."

"Then why'd you call him? Surely it was to confront him about something."

"Calling someone ain't a crime. It certainly doesn't equate to murder."

"That doesn't answer my question."

"What's going on?" Henry's voice boomed across the pavement.

Kevin sighed in relief. "Finally! Can you please get this old lady to move? This is my rental and she refuses to get out of the way."

"Emma?" Henry raised his eyebrows.

Emma knew she needed to get Kevin to admit to the murder quickly. She unlocked Alexander's phone screen and held it up to Henry. "Kevin's cell was the last known number to call Alexander before his death. His brother's death was linked to a mistake Alexander may have made. And his wife was having an affair with Alexander, so there are two possible motives. Add in his threat, which multiple people overheard, and the fact his car was seen stalking me and Amber and in the driveway this morning as well as the morning of Alexander's death. It's all highly suspect. I know you'd agree, Henry. The least you can do is get a warrant to search his property."

Henry sighed. "How did you get Alexander's phone?" He took the phone and hit the number Amber had highlighted. Kevin's cell began to ring, which Kevin quickly silenced.

Henry sighed again.

"Calling someone doesn't equate to murder." Kevin stiffened.

"Why did you call him?" Henry asked.

Kevin hesitated, his lips pressing into a thin line. "I—well." His gaze darted between them. "I don't have to answer that. You know this won't hold up in court."

Henry ignored him. "Where were you on June twenty-fifth between five and seven p.m.?" he asked, referencing the time Emma had shown up complaining of being stalked.

Kevin's stance relaxed as he pulled out his phone, flipping through photos. "Here." He turned the screen toward Henry, showing a series of images from a formal dinner party. The time stamps and location data were visible. "Work event. I wasn't even in town. I left my car here and flew back just for the day."

Henry studied the evidence before shooting Emma a pointed look. "Come on, let the man into his room. He's done nothing wrong."

"There could be an explanation. Maybe the photos are doctored. Maybe someone's working with him." *Like Chad Monroe.*

"Go home to your husband, Emma. Don't make me arrest you for breach of the peace. What you're doing is unlawful. I don't even want to know how you got Alexander's phone." Henry took her by the arm rather forcibly and began to lead her away.

Emma caught sight of Susan in that moment, watching from the sidewalk. Her pudgy poodle was pulling at the leash as she stayed stagnant, squinting in Emma's direction.

Great. If she's anything like her mother, this will spread like wildfire.

Emma pulled from Henry's grip. "I'm going," she said with a grumble, holding back on telling him how, if he'd just do his job, she wouldn't have to.

Chapter Twenty

Emma was lying in bed with a book hiding her face. She wasn't really reading it, just looking at the words and hoping Tim wouldn't say anything. Surely, by now, word would've spread.

Tim came to the other side of the bed. The mattress sunk as he slid onto his side. He cleared his throat, but Emma just turned the page.

"Ems, do you want to tell me what happened today?"

"I went to check on Amber. She was fine. They didn't even enter the house."

"And after that?"

Emma shrugged.

Tim's body sinking further into the mattress made Emma feel lightheaded.

"Henry called me. He said you confronted Kevin Hedwink and accused him of murdering Alexander."

"Well, all the signs point to that." She flipped a page.

"Did you have Amber's permission to confiscate Alexander's phone, or did you take that initiative on your own?"

Emma bit her lip, which told Tim everything.

"How'd you manage to bypass the password?"

"Chloe helped with that."

Tim banged the back of his head against the headboard. "You have our granddaughter involved now?" He groaned and rubbed between his eyes. "It's bad enough stealing phones and reading private messages—illegal and unethical. But to get your underaged granddaughter involved in your crimes? Really, Ems?! What were you thinking?"

"I was *thinking* that if the police won't act, someone has to before someone else gets killed. And Chloe? She was going to get involved regardless. This way, I can at least keep tabs on her."

Tim sighed. He looked over toward the window. It was a foggy night, but a few stars persisted.

"I know you're just trying to help, and I agree that something does seem fishy, but I'm concerned. You're becoming reckless, Ems. Confronting Kevin openly like that was positively dangerous."

"We were in the open. He would've had a hard time killing me in broad daylight without someone noticing."

Tim shook his head. "Please, for me." He took her book, laid it in her lap and took her hands in his. "Please drop it."

Emma met his eyes. He was begging her with that gaze of his like a sad little puppy. Normally she wouldn't be able to resist, but she had fallen too deep. She couldn't just retreat now.

"I can't," she whispered. "I'm so close, Tim."

A tear slid down her cheek and dangled off her jawline.

He sighed, his gaze dropping to her lap, where the book lay open—untouched, unread. "Then stay safe. No more confronting people in the open. Whatever you find, take it straight to Henry."

Emma exhaled, staring up at the ceiling before lifting the book back to her nose. "Fine."

Emma did her best to ignore the stares and hushed whispers that followed her through the dining room.

"Everyone's being weird," Chloe whispered as they walked side-by-side to the kitchen.

"Yeah, they all must've heard about my confrontation with Kevin."

"Yeah, didn't sound like it went too well," Chloe said, referencing the recording she had listened to. "It could be Chad. Maybe Kevin was the one he was talking to over the phone. If they're friends, Chad could've used his car to drive Kevin to the airport and then taken it to spy on Amber."

"So, you think it's Monroe?"

"Could've been both of them. Who knows?"

Emma walked over to turn the stove down before her pot of eggs boiled over. "Why would either of them go after Amber, though?"

Chloe shrugged. "Maybe they think she knows something, or maybe she influenced her husband to make whatever decision he made. I don't think it's too far-fetched for a wife to convince her husband to cover up some mistake at work that could threaten his career and good name."

Emma shook her head. "I can't see Amber meddling in Alexander's affairs, but you could be right. There could be more than just one murderer."

Chloe filled the tray with another cut of French toast casserole and two cups of coffee. "Table six?"

"Yes," Emma said.

Just as Emma was tidying up the kitchen, Amber entered through the back door. Emma was surprised to see her. She hadn't visited the B&B since Alexander's death.

Emma could tell by her frown that she wasn't in the best mood, but she chose not to focus on it.

"Amber, it's so good to see you. Can I whip you up something?"

Amber took a seat across the counter, just like she always did. "I should've just called," she said with a sigh, looking around the kitchen. "But," she sighed again. "I heard some things and thought in-person would be better to discuss it."

"What's bothering you?" Emma placed a teacup with hot chamomile in front of her friend.

Amber didn't even look down at it. "Did you confront that guy—uh, Kevin—about murdering Alexander?"

Emma sat on the other side. She poured herself a cup of tea as well and warmed her hands on it. "I did."

"And you got my husband's phone somehow and showed it to him?"

Emma raised her eyebrows. What, did Susan have binoculars? But she wasn't too surprised. This little town had a way of finding out the smallest details.

"Kevin was one of the last people to have called him."

"So, you stole my husband's phone and you've been conducting an investigation without telling me?" Amber looked to the ceiling, trying to keep her tears from colliding with the flour-dusted counter.

"I didn't want to trouble you, but I—I was worried, especially after that incident at the beach. If there is a murderer out there, you might be in danger, Amber. I can't lose you. You're my best friend."

Amber groaned and turned her face to the window overlooking the garden. "This morning, at the grocers, Anne approached me, asking what I thought—if I suspected murder, too. Any conversation with Alexander as the subject is a burden, but that was icing on the cake. I just want to forget it—all of it. Suicide, murder—it doesn't matter. He's dead. And you need to stop. I need you to stop. Not just for my sake but for yours. You're the laughing-stock of the town right now. If only you could hear what people are saying about you! And this—this is drawing all eyes on me too, and I just...I can't. I can't cope with it."

"Amber, I know you want to forget, but forgetting isn't going to help you heal..." Emma reached to hold her hand, but Amber pulled back.

"I'd like his phone back."

Emma got up and walked over to her purse that hung on the hook by the door. "Sure." She pulled the phone out and slid it to Amber.

Amber stared at it for a long time before lifting it with trembling fingers and hiding it away in her bag.

"I'm sorry Anne brought up Alexander, but I think trying to forget isn't going to help."

"You cannot tell me how to grieve, how to heal." Amber raised her voice till it was a shrill screech. "I am the one with a dead husband; I am the one who has to live with it. Stop playing your detective games! This is serious, and it's not about you this time."

Chloe came through the swaying doors with an empty tray but slowly backed out when she saw Amber losing it. Amber turned to the noise, though. She rubbed at her puffy eyes and pulled her bag up over her shoulder.

"Amber." Emma grabbed her arm. "I care so much." Tears collected in her eyes. "This isn't a game. I'm just trying to keep you safe."

"That's Henry's job, not yours." Amber yanked away and walked to the door, slamming it so hard it did a double flip back and forth before settling.

Emma leaned against the counter, gripping it with paling hands. The room was spinning and her heart was pounding so hard against her chest, she felt breathless.

What am I doing? Do I really think I can solve a murder? Maybe Amber and Tim are right. I'm in over my head. This isn't my job. Maybe all I'm doing is pushing those I love far away.

Chloe entered with an empty tray. "Table seven needs some water." She grabbed the water pitcher and put it on her tray. "You okay?"

"I'm fine." Emma pushed a stray hair under her netted cap.

"Amber might be mad at you right now, but when you solve the murder, it'll be worth it," Chloe said.

"Maybe we shouldn't try." Emma sucked in a breath. "Maybe she's right. We have no idea what we're doing. And it isn't just Amber who's upset with me; Tim is, too. He thinks what we've been doing—hacking phones and things, is unethical."

Chloe shrugged. "Well, fine, then we can just be more ethical about it."

"I'm worried I'm putting you at risk."

"I'd do it without you and you know it," Chloe said, turning to leave before Emma could say anything more.

Chapter Twenty-One

Chloe walked down the uneven sidewalk leading to the lake. It wasn't exactly the most relaxing walk. Afternoons were always busy, and she kept having to make space for the group of tourists that would pass her, dodging their swinging tote bags and beach umbrellas.

A small child in swim trunks and a towel wrapped around his neck nearly tripped her as he rushed by, screaming about catching the biggest wave, not that there were many waves today. The lake was quite calm—only ripples graced the surface today.

She crossed the street toward the ice cream van and small chocolate shop. It was quieter on that side of the road, a little further away from the main attraction—the lake.

Chloe didn't really know where she was going. She was just killing time, as they say, while simultaneously wondering who the killer was. Maybe Chad, maybe Kevin…

But just as she was rounding the bend, she spotted Amber at a picnic table outside the local bar, sitting across from none other than Chad Monroe. Chloe went down an alleyway and came back up along the side of the building, hidden in the shadows, but close enough to hear what was being said.

Granny Em didn't see Amber as a suspect, but Chloe did. Alexander was Amber's husband and she seemed distraught over the whole thing, but that didn't excuse her from Chloe's list. She had a motive. Her husband was cheating, and it was very possible she found out. Jared had said he heard her run outside to look for Alexander. She was his wife. She probably knew the exact route he'd take. It would've been easy for her to find and kill him where it was most isolated, then get home in time to clean herself up.

Chloe didn't want to make her out to be a suspect, of course. She liked Amber. She felt bad for her. But someone had left a threatening note, seeming to blame her for it. Had they seen it happen? Was it blackmail? Was this why Amber was so upset when she found out Emma was investigating the murder? Most wives would want justice for their husbands. But Amber just wanted to forget hers altogether. Why?

"You're holding up well," Chad said.

Amber sighed loudly. "What's the real reason for wanting to see me, Chad? I know it's not because you care for my loss. You and Alexander were hardly close."

"Right." Chad cleared his throat. "I loaned Alexander something of mine and was wondering if I could come and look for it. I imagine you wouldn't know where it is, so I could save you the trouble…"

"What is it?" Her tone was sharp.

"Uh, work-related."

Amber shook her head wildly, smacking herself with her hair. "That isn't an answer."

"A USB." His hand shook, and he quickly pulled his sleeve over it. "Or a disc. Look, I'll pay you if you want."

"I don't need your money. Alexander left me plenty, but even if he didn't, I still wouldn't take a dime from you or anybody."

"Then what can I give you?"

"Nothing." She stood abruptly and slapped a twenty-dollar bill on the table. "Bye, Chad."

Amber stormed off, her sundress flying in the wind. Chad pulled out his phone, looking like he was about to call someone, but just as quickly, he shoved it back into his pocket.

Chloe remembered what Jared had said about Alexander looking for something. Was it the same thing Chad was looking for? What could be on that disc that's so important?

Chapter Twenty-Two

Emma sat at a small round table on her porch, gazing out at the lake. She had chosen a secluded spot in the far corner, away from the gossiping women rocking in their chairs near the entrance. Across from her, Silvia sipped on chamomile tea.

"Have you spoken to Amber recently?" Silvia asked.

"Not since we argued." Emma sighed, dipping her soaked tea bag in and out till the steaming water was the perfect shade. "I just feel so torn."

"I'm shocked, to be fair." Silvia smoothed out the napkin on her lap. "I didn't expect you to take initiative in solving a murder."

"Do you judge me for it, too?"

Silvia's lips curled into a wry smile. "No. I'm just impressed you've managed to dig up clues while running this place. I don't know how you juggle it all. I couldn't dream of it. Though," she shrugged, "I suppose my dreams have always been smaller. I was just a mom, and now I'm a grandmother."

"Just a mom?" Emma scoffed. "You raised seven kids and homeschooled them! I always admired you for that." Her gaze drifted toward the lake, then up to her daughter's old bedroom window.

"Well, it was my retirement plan," Silvia teased, stirring in a splash of cream and honey. "With seven of them, I figured at least one would take me in when I'm too old to live on my own." She smiled wistfully. "Those days felt endless sometimes, but I miss them now. I'm sure you can relate."

Emma thought of her daughter when she was little and still wanted to spend time with her. Emma had been her world. How different things were now. "I do."

"But at least we get to relive it a little with our grandkids," Silvia said. "Chloe is the spitting image of Bella."

Emma swallowed a hot mouthful of tea. "She is. They are so alike—determined as anything and absolute spit-fires." She smiled. "I just hope they know how much I love them."

"I'm sure they do." Silvia tucked a strand of dark hair behind her ear. Her bracelet jingled in the wind as she looked around. "So, a murderer in our midst—in this town?"

Emma gave a half smile. "You think I'm crazy?"

"It's just wild. But I can believe it. I knew Alexander well enough to know he would never have killed himself. So, what's your next move?"

"I'm not sure. I feel like I'm at a standstill right now. Chloe did overhear a conversation between Chad and Amber the other day, where Chad asked for a disc or USB. Maybe I'll go visit Amber to apologize."

"And look for it?"

"I'm not sure if I should…or where I'd even begin to look."

"Maybe you could ask Jared. He knew Alexander inside and out. If anyone knew where Alexander hid something, it would be him."

Emma thought back to how Jared had said Alexander had torn his office apart looking for something, so it seemed reasonable that maybe the disc went missing for him, too. If Chad or Kevin hadn't taken it, that led to only two others who could have—Jared or Amber. Emma couldn't see Amber doing anything like that, but she didn't know Jared well enough to say he wouldn't, and Jared did clean the house, so he could've easily swiped it. But why? He was just the butler…tending to a mansion he now owned.

Chapter Twenty-Three

Chloe looked through the library archives, filtering through the old newspapers, and came across one featuring the Kirk mansion.

'Tragedy Averted,' it read. Chloe clicked on the article and zoomed in. The picture was of Alexander and Jared when they were just boys—maybe nine or ten.

She skimmed through the article. Alexander Kirk, age nine, nearly drowned after falling out of his kayak and hitting his head. Luckily, his friend, Jared, came to the rescue and pulled him to safety.

Maybe this is why he left him his house—a payment for saving his life. Or was it more sinister? Chloe shook her head. *Trying to solve a murder really does have you thinking the worst of people.*

Chloe's phone buzzed, and she looked down to see a text from Emma. '*You want to tag along to Amber's? I was going to apologize. Maybe you could chat with Jared and see if he knows anything about that missing USB.*'

Chloe texted back. '*Sure. Pick me up at the library.*'

Chloe snapped a picture of the article and slid her phone into her back pocket. The librarian smiled at her as she walked past her to the double doors.

It was a sweltering, humid day, but at least there was a breeze to keep it from feeling too suffocating. Chloe shifted on the curb, waiting for Emma's truck to pull in. Her mind wandered back to Amber. She had been so distraught when she called, convinced Alexander was dead. But how could she have known that?

Maybe it was just a gut feeling, but even that seemed strange. When she and Granny Em had gone to pick Amber up, Alexander wouldn't have been that late yet. Why jump straight to the worst-case scenario? It would have made more sense to assume he had stopped for coffee or ran into someone he knew.

Maybe Jared could answer more than just the mystery of the missing USB. Maybe he could explain how Amber had known.

The familiar rumble of an engine snapped Chloe from her thoughts.

"Hop in!" Granny Em called through the open window as she pulled up to the curb.

Chloe swung open the door and climbed into the passenger seat of Pop's truck.

"Find anything important?" Granny Em asked.

Chloe gave a half-shrug. "Just an old newspaper article about Jared saving Alexander's life when they were kids. Apparently, Alexander almost drowned."

Granny Em's fingers tightened around the steering wheel. "That would explain the will."

"Maybe."

The Kirk mansion sat on the hill, the tip of the roof touching a layer of fogged clouds. Chloe followed Granny Em up the marble steps, through the double doors, and into the spacious entryway.

"Amber is just upstairs in the library," Jared explained, gesturing with the flick of a wrist which way that was.

"Thanks, Jared." Granny Em headed down the hall, but Chloe stayed behind.

"Could I talk to you about something?" she asked Jared.

His peppered mustache lifted as he smiled. "Certainly." He walked toward the kitchen. "Care for a cup of tea? I just made a pot of Earl Grey."

"Sure, thanks." Chloe followed him down the hall, looking at the newly sanded, polished wood floor under her feet. It was a stark contrast to the wood floors of her grandmother's B&B.

She walked through an oval arch and into the kitchen. Besides a cut in the wall where an old phone would have sat, everything was fresh and modern—white-painted cabinets, stainless steel appliances, marble countertops.

Jared gathered two cups and placed them delicately on a side table by a partially open window.

The smell of the beach wafted through the crack as Chloe sat down and sipped on her hot tea.

"Cream? Sugar?" Jared pushed the saucer toward her.

She shook her head. "I'm good."

"So, what did you need to pick my brain about?" he asked, looking into Chloe's blue eyes.

"Uh, well, I think I know what that burglar wanted. I overheard a conversation between Chad Monroe and Amber—please don't tell her—and he wanted a USB or disc where some information was stored. Do you know where Alexander would've kept that?"

Jared's lips twitched, and he turned his gaze to the window. "I do," he answered, taking a sip of tea.

"You do?" Chloe nearly jumped from the excitement. *This was too easy.* "Where is it?"

"My bedroom." He looked back over at her. "I took it."

"Why did you do that?"

"I knew what was on it, but I wasn't sure what to do about it. Alexander was my friend, but what he had done was…wrong, and this was proof of his and Chad Monroe's wrongdoing. I didn't know what to do—keep it or turn it in to the police. When he died, though." He shrugged. "I don't know. Amber has been through so much. The last thing she needs is me opening this can of worms."

"What's on it?"

"A conversation between Chad Monroe and Alexander in which they both acknowledge the safety issues of the ship but mutually agree to do nothing about it. I imagine Alexander kept it in case Monroe tried to turn the blame exclusively on him if things went wrong, which they did. Hundreds of sailors died because of their negligence."

"Do you think Chad killed him, then, to try and keep him quiet?"

"I don't know." Jared's body was as stiff as a board.

Did you kill him? Chloe asked inwardly. *You knew he committed these crimes. Maybe you thought he deserved to die.*

"I can give you the USB if you think it will help in uncovering who may have murdered him. I had assumed it was suicide, guilt from his crimes, maybe fear because I took the evidence unbeknownst to him and he felt the reveal was impending. I blamed myself then, but now I'm beginning to agree that someone may have killed him."

"Thanks. Yeah, that would be useful." Chloe rubbed her knuckles. She remembered she had wanted to ask about Amber. She looked to the archway. The hallway was still empty, but she didn't know how much time she'd have before Granny Em and Amber would show. "Regarding the morning of his death, my grandmother said Amber claimed she knew Alexander was dead—like a premonition. I just, I don't know. I was wondering what you remembered from that morning and if there was anything that would explain how she'd know that."

Jared raised an eyebrow. "Amber couldn't have killed him, if that's what you're suggesting."

"I'm not…I…Well, why do you say that?"

"She loved him to folly. She knew he was having an affair, and she ignored it, hoping he'd amend his ways of his own accord. I never knew a more devoted wife."

"She knew?"

He nodded. "Yes, she confided her suspicions to me, and I confirmed them. I knew, too. Alexander was hardly secretive about it. He thought—" Jared cleared his throat and quickly went quiet.

"Having tea without me, Jared?" Amber flitted in. Her tone was oddly light.

Granny Em walked in behind her. She looked pleased, so Chloe assumed the apology went well.

Jared stood and pulled out a couple more chairs from the table. "Please, there's enough for all of us. I will fetch some biscuits from the pantry."

Just before he headed toward the pantry, his eyes met Chloe's. Chloe looked over at Amber. So, she had known all along. But she stayed because she loved him to folly. But what can such folly do to a person?

Chapter Twenty-Four

Emma sat in front of the police station, the USB snug in her purse. Jared had shared his hesitation with her. This could go public. This could open new wounds for Amber. But it would also prove that both Chad Monroe and Kevin Hedwink had a reason for wanting Alexander dead.

"They probably won't do anything," she muttered as she opened the door.

The room smelled like disinfectant, like a hospital would. Emma strode to the front desk where Amy stood, dressed in a freshly ironed blue uniform. Emma smiled at her, but Amy stayed stone-faced.

"I have evidence with a note explaining what's on it." Emma retrieved the USB and note from her purse. "Please hand it to Henry. I think once he opens it, it'll be self-explanatory."

Amy moved robotically, picking up the USB and note. "Thanks. I'll be sure to get it to him."

Emma could see past the politeness. Amy must think her a real quack. Probably inwardly laughing at her behind that blank face of hers. Oh well. Sooner or later, everyone would know the truth—Emma was sure of it.

"Hear anything from Henry?" Chloe asked. She was standing by the sink, washing some lettuce for a salad.

"Not yet." Emma opened the fridge and stared at the near-empty shelves. "I'm missing the tomatoes," she said. "Why don't you cut the lettuce and peel the carrots? I'll be back in no time."

"Sure thing." Chloe opened a drawer and fetched the peeler. She knew where everything was now—something not even Tim did.

Emma grabbed the keys from her purse; they jingled against her wrist as she headed toward the car. Seagulls cawed and flew above her. Their wings were a blur of fluttering white against the blue sky.

Emma opened the car door and pushed her keys into the ignition. The engine roared to life. She gripped the wheel and backed out. A few old ladies watched and waved at her from the porch as she drove off. Everyone recognized Emma's car since she had had it for over a decade now. She patted the dashboard with one of her hands. Tim was always getting on her case for driving this old thing, but she didn't see any reason to upgrade. It made weird noises on occasion, but it got her from point A to point B just fine and that was the important thing.

She drove down the road toward an empty intersection. She applied pressure to the brakes as she neared the stop sign, but it was like pushing on air.

Her car wasn't slowing down. If anything, it was speeding up.

"What on earth!" Emma slammed her foot on the pedal again. "Come on, work!"

She grabbed the emergency brake and pulled—slowly, steadily, just like Tim had taught her. But no luck.

The stop sign was a blur of red as she sped by it. Her breaths came out in short gasps.

She looked around frantically. *What to do? What to do?*

The hill leading up to Amber's house came into her line of vision. She yanked the wheel and headed toward it.

"Please work. Please work." She really didn't need to ruin Amber's day by driving straight into her living room.

To her relief, the car slowed.

Everything felt frozen, including her. Emma couldn't even feel her body at first. She stared blankly ahead at the untouched mansion, its garden peeking out from behind the fence and the stairs twisting down toward the beach. Slowly, her gaze dropped to her white-knuckled hands, gripping the wheel.

"I'm alive," she whispered, her voice trembling as much as her hands. In a whirlwind, the scenes of what had just transpired flashed through her mind. She let go of the wheel and fumbled for her phone.

Her fingers shook as she dialed Tim's number. Each ring sounded distant, muffled, like it was coming from underwater.

"Hey, Ems," Tim answered, his casual tone a lifeline.

"Tim." Her voice cracked, breathless and thin. "I—I need you to come get me. The brakes… they're not working."

"What?!"

His raised voice nearly sent her spiralling back into a panic.

"I'm okay. I've stopped. Luckily, Amber's hill did the trick at slowing me down."

Tim sighed. "Thank God. Stay put. I'll be right over."

Emma clicked the phone shut and leaned back against the leather seat.

It seemed to take ages for Tim to show. Emma had left her car and sat in the grass, still feeling numb and paralyzed.

"Ems!" Tim jumped out of his truck before even shutting it off. He ran to her and gathered her in his burly arms. "You alright?" His lips pushed against her cheek, but she barely felt them.

"Just in shock, I think. I-I tried the emergency brake, but even that didn't work."

"It didn't?" Tim's eyebrows shot up, and he looked back at her car. "That should've worked. Those are two different systems—unlikely for them both to fail at the same time."

She could see the gears turning in his head. If she were in a better frame of mind, she would have been able to guess exactly what he was thinking. But everything was a blur—even her thoughts.

"All right." He touched her cheek with his palm. "Let's get you home. I've already called the tow truck. I can let Jared know, and he will instruct them on where to go. We don't need to stick around."

"Okay." She let him help her up and leaned against him as he led her to the truck.

"I love you, Ems. More than you will ever know," he said as he kissed the top of her head. "I'm mighty glad you're unharmed."

Chapter Twenty-Five

Emma sat on the porch steps of her B&B, looking across the parking lot toward the blue stretch of water. Grey clouds were coming in from the north. Soon, there'd be rain. She could already feel the humidity on her skin.

The door swung open and shut, and Tim came to sit beside her.

"I just got off the phone with the mechanic," he said. His jaw was set tight. "It wasn't an accident, Ems. Someone cut both brake lines."

Emma hugged her knees. She knew accusing Kevin would come back to bite her, but she hadn't expected the murderer to go after her, especially not with everyone thinking her a crazy old bat. "I must be close," she whispered.

"Close?!" Tim groaned and rubbed his eyes. "Someone tried to kill you! I don't care how close you are, this needs to end. Please. I cannot lose you. I can't." His arms shook.

Emma grabbed his hand and settled it on her knees. Then she looked into Tim's chestnut eyes. "I know you're scared. I am too. But I won't be safe until this murderer is found. I know it. You know it. I can say I'll stop all you want, but will he believe it? I've already gone public. I can't reverse it now."

Tim bit his bottom lip and looked at his boots. "I'm coming with you, then, everywhere. To the grocery store, to Amber's, everywhere."

"That's a bit much, don't you think?" She smiled sideways at him.

"I need to be there to keep you safe."

She touched his cheek. "And who will run the B&B with both of us absent?"

"Well, you'll just have to figure that part out now, won't you? Because I'd rather this place burn to the ground than lose the woman I've loved these forty-odd years."

Emma just sat there, looking out toward the lake, feeling the tremors of her husband's hand on her knee. "I guess I'll give Silvia a call, then."

Chloe was sitting at the front desk when Emma re-entered with Tim. The lounge was unusually empty.

"Anyone call?" Emma asked.

Chloe shook her head. "It's been dead." She gave Emma a once over. "Not an accident, huh?"

"Nope. The mechanic confirmed it was sabotage."

Chloe sucked back a breath. "I'm glad you're okay. Guess we just need to find the killer before he strikes again."

Emma pinched her lips. "I think it's best if I handle it alone from here on out. You've been a huge help, but it's getting too dangerous. I can't risk you becoming the next target. In fact…" She hesitated. "I think I should call your mother. I can't let you stay if it means putting you in harm's way."

Chloe shot to her feet, hands gripping the corners of the desk. "You can't! This isn't fair! I won't let you send me back."

"Chloe." Emma sighed loudly. "You know I've enjoyed your company and your help and I love you—dearly. But this is for your safety."

"I don't want to go back. I want to stay here—with you. You're more of a mother to me than she is." Tears began to cradle Chloe's pale face. Her chin trembled and her hands shook like falling leaves. "But of course…everyone always sends me away."

"Like I said, this is me trying to protect you. I can't have you get hurt." Emma reached for Chloe's arm, but she pulled away.

"Sure. Tell yourself that." Her voice cracked as she spun on her heels and rushed up the stairs.

Emma pulled her frizzy grey hair back into a messy bun. She sighed, the tightness in her chest increasing with every breath. "I can't do anything right, it seems."

Tim squeezed her shoulder. "Give her time. She'll come to her senses, eventually."

Emma sat in the comfort of her kitchen, inhaling the scent of freshly ground coffee beans. She stared at Bella's number on her phone before finally hitting the green 'call' button.

"What is it?" Bella asked in a sour tone.

Emma sighed, rubbing her fingers against her temple. "I'm calling about Chloe. We love having her. She's been no trouble, but there's a safety concern. It seems like there's a murderer targeting me."

Bella's laughter was sharp and dismissive. "Is this your idea of a prank? Did Chloe put you up to it?"

"I'm being serious. Someone sabotaged my car. I could've died. I don't want Chloe caught up in this. I think it may be best to cut her visit short. Tim could drive her back as early as tomorrow."

"Tomorrow? Are you serious?" Bella groaned loudly. "You can't just dump her back on me. I'm not even home—I'm in B.C. at a cooking convention. And I'm not cutting my trip short because of your paranoia. Honestly, Chloe's probably safer there in the middle of nowhere than she is in Toronto. Just last week, there was a hit-and-run by her school. Week before that, someone broke into the bakery down the street. If safety's your concern, trust me—she's better off with you."

Emma pinched the bridge of her nose. "What if I flew her out to B.C.? Tim and I might be able to make that work."

Bella's frustrated groan echoed through the line. "Mom, enough. You agreed to take her for the summer. If you couldn't handle it, you shouldn't have volunteered."

The line went dead, and Emma lowered the phone to her lap. She sighed, looking out the window at the garden where her daughter used to play. Where had she gone wrong?

Tim walked in. "What'd she say?"

Emma looked up at him. "She's away at a cooking convention. It looks like we'll have to figure something else out."

"Poor girl." Tim sighed, opening the cupboards and rifling through them till he reached his favorite cookies. "I'd suggest taking her camping, but I can't leave you here by yourself. I mean, I guess there's no real threat to Chloe yet, right? You've just had her doing the behind-the-scenes?"

"She's spoken to Jared, but I think that's it, so unless he's the murderer…"

Tim snorted. "Jared? Sabotage a car? The man doesn't look like he could fix a broken toaster, let alone mess with a vehicle."

Emma shrugged, a faint smile tugging at her lips. "The internet can teach you a lot these days."

"Does he even know how to use it?"

Emma laughed. Jared did strike her as someone stuck in generations past. "Maybe, but you're right. He's probably harmless."

"I doubt we have anything to worry about. You made a public show of yourself. Luckily, Chloe hasn't. I'll keep an eye on her, but I think it's safe to assume you're the only one in the line of fire."

Chapter Twenty-Six

Chloe lay curled up in bed, knees tucked tightly to her chest. The faint glow of her bedside lamp illuminated the scattered papers and notes spread out across the comforter. She'd been up all night, going over the list of suspects again and again, her mind racing with possibilities. She had to figure this out before her grandmother sent her away. She just had to.

It wasn't just about not wanting to go home—though the thought of returning to her cold, empty house made her stomach twist. She'd always known this stay was temporary. But leaving now, with so much unresolved, felt like abandonment. She couldn't leave Granny Em in harm's way, not when danger was closing in.

Time was running out. The killer knew her grandmother was onto them. If Chloe left now, anything could happen. And she didn't think she could live with herself if she wasn't here to stop it.

A soft knock on the door jarred her from her thoughts.

"You awake?" It was her grandmother's voice.

"What do you want?" Chloe tried to keep her voice steady, but it was useless. It just sounded like a perpetual broken record.

"I just wanted to let you know you can stay for now on the condition that you don't go off anywhere alone or draw attention to yourself."

Chloe rubbed her puffy eyes. "You mean it?" she asked, her voice lightening.

"I mean it. Now shut off that light and get some sleep already. We have a crime to solve and we'll need our wits about us."

Granny Em was on the phone when Chloe entered the kitchen, steps dragging as she fought the exhaustion from only a couple hours of sleep. Still, she was ready to help with whatever needed baking.

"Yeah, okay, run the ad. It's probably a blessing in disguise," Granny Em said, balancing the phone with one hand while flipping a pancake with the other. "Like you've been telling me all along, I can't keep doing this solo. Thanks, Silvia. You're a lifesaver. Bye."

Chloe sank onto the stool across the counter, resting her chin in her hand. "What was that about?"

Granny Em set the pancake onto a plate and glanced at Chloe, a small smile tugging at her lips. "Silvia's helping me round up some help—an extra cook, a secretary, a waitress, a housekeeper, even a gardener. It'll mean raising my prices, but it's long overdue. I just hope my regulars won't be too upset."

"What brought this on?"

Granny Em leaned against the counter, her smile turning sly. "Tim, of course. He won't let me keep up my detective work without tagging along now, and I can't let the B&B fall apart while we're off investigating. For years, it's been just me or him running the place. But now…" She hesitated, her fingers tapping lightly on the counter. "Now, I'll have to trust someone else to step in. It's a little nerve-wracking, handing over even a part of it, but I don't see another option."

"I'm sure it'll work out." Chloe yawned into her elbow.

"You should go back to sleep. As much as I appreciate it, I can survive without your help, you know." Granny Em pushed a strand of hair behind Chloe's ear and tapped her cheek. "I need you alert in case some big clue crops up."

Chloe looked over at the swinging doors. She had spotted Chad Monroe before coming in, sitting in his usual corner and sipping his black coffee as he read the paper.

Granny Em had just turned in the USB that had incriminating evidence against him. What if he had seen her at the station and connected the dots? What if he was the killer? Chloe felt she'd be far better off observing him than sleeping.

"I'm not old, you know." Chloe grabbed her apron off the hook on the wall and tied it around her waist. "I've gotten far less sleep than this before and managed just fine—even scoring an A on my algebra test."

"If you insist." Granny Em slid the hot pancakes onto two thick plates and put them on the tray for Chloe to carry out. "Table nine."

Table nine ended up being Julia's table. Usually Susan ate with her, but it was just Julia today. She was looking at herself with her phone camera flipped around, applying another layer of that brilliantly bright lipstick of hers.

"Good morning!" Chloe faked a chirpy demeanor. "Here are your pancakes." Julia hardly looked up at her. "Thanks," she mumbled, setting her phone beside her empty coffee mug. Chloe could see the notification of an unread text from Chad Monroe that started with, 'You're unhinged.' She looked over at his table across the room. Why would Julia be texting Monroe? And why would he make that remark? Was she on to him, too? It would make sense. She also suspected Alexander had been killed. Maybe she knew who it was—that it was Monroe.

"Can I help you?" Julia looked up with a grimace.

Chloe fumbled with her tray. "Uh, do you need syrup or anything? More coffee? I see it's empty."

Julia looked at the full serving of maple syrup on her table with a raised brow, then her empty cup. "Yeah, sure, just half a cup."

"I'll be right back," Chloe said, scampering back to the kitchen. "You won't believe what I accidentally saw on Julia's cell," she said.

Granny Em's eyebrows rose. "What did you see?"

"A text from Chad Monroe asking her if she was unhinged. I wonder if maybe she's onto him, just like we are."

"Hmmm."

"Maybe I should see if he needs more coffee too," Chloe said, grabbing the French press.

Granny Em held up her hand. "No. I'll go. You serve Julia, and remember—stay in the shadows. They know I'm looking for the killer, but you should be safe. Let's keep it that way."

Chapter Twenty-Seven

Emma walked over to Chad with a hot pot of coffee. "Need a refill?" she asked.

He looked up at her, leaned back and smiled as if they were good friends. "You are mighty good at reading minds," he said, pushing his mug toward her.

"How are you holding up since Alexander's death?" Emma asked in a casual tone as she filled his cup to the brim, knowing he never took cream.

"It's been strange. I'll admit, some days I expect to see him across the table."

"Do you really think he committed suicide?" Emma watched his mannerisms for any tells.

"I know you don't." He smirked.

"I guess it's all over town, then?"

"Yeah, poor Kev."

"You know him?"

"Why do you say that?"

"Well, 'Kev' is a bit too casual for someone who doesn't."

"You catch on to every detail, don't you?" He blew on his coffee before taking a sip. "I do know him a bit. His brother was under my charge. He, uh, died in an accident—something Kevin blamed Alexander for. I take it you know this, though?"

"I do."

Monroe nodded. "I was here to investigate the matter, off-record, of course. Kevin wasn't supposed to show up, but, as you have it…" He lifted his mug toward Julia's table. "His wife knew Alexander too. Funny how small the world can be sometimes."

"I take it you know her, too, now."

"Now I do. I made sure to make her acquaintance after Alexander's death. She's trying to find his murderer, too." He took another sip of hot coffee. "At least, I assume that's why she's been stalking me."

"Stalking you? Are you sure?"

"At the grocery store, she's just down the aisle. I go fishing at the lake and spot her just within view, staring right at me. That wouldn't be so bad, of course, but I found a note the other day equivalent to 'I know what you did this summer'."

Emma glanced back at Julia. *Did she leave the note on Amber's car?*

"I didn't do it." Chad wiped his beard with his napkin. "I saw enough death during my time in the navy. I'd never add to the list purposefully."

Emma's lips thinned. *Even if he had incriminating evidence linking you to a whole slew of murders?*

"Of course not."

Emma sat across from the first interviewee. She was young, maybe nineteen, with red curly hair and freckles that could very well be making her appear younger than she really was. Her resume was hardly impressive, but she lived a town over, so she had that going for her. The last thing Emma wanted was to hire a local and then have to fire them a week later because it wasn't working out. Her reputation was already on the hook as it was.

"So, Ashley, what experience do you have cooking?"

"Call me Ash." The girl smiled, red curls framing her pudgy face. "It's easier."

"Okay, Ash," Emma replied, forcing a smile and glancing down at her mostly empty resume. It only listed experience as a cashier; nothing related to cooking, but that wasn't a deal-breaker. Emma knew the home was the best place to learn how to cook.

"Uh, I don't have any formal experience, but I really enjoy it. I'm good at it, too. I don't burn anything, and it always tastes good. Of course, I don't have any references you can call to confirm that besides my mom and little brother. But this is my dream, if that counts for anything."

Emma smiled a genuine smile. "It does." She highlighted Ashley's name on the resume. She knew she should interview others first—that would be the prudent thing, but a young woman claiming cooking was her dream brought back memories.

Even if she wasn't the best cook, how hard was it to follow a recipe? Passion was worth far more than skill as far as Emma was concerned.

"All right, when can you start?"

"What? Really?" She nearly jumped out of her chair.

Emma closed the folder that had the other resumes in it. *I guess I'll have a lot of canceling to do.* "Really."

"Uh, today, I guess."

"Perfect. Let me show you around. If you don't mind, I may need you at the front desk too, just for today."

Ash looked nervous. "Oh, I'm not the best at speaking."

Emma touched her shoulder. "I'll give you a script for answering the phones. And it's just temporary. I have some errands I need to run today, and I can't leave the desk empty."

"Uh, okay. I guess if you give me something to read off, it should be easy enough." Ash rubbed her forearm as she followed Emma to the kitchen.

"This will be your home from seven to noon, noon to two, and five to seven," Emma said, gesturing to the cabinets and stove. "If you have a cellphone, I can send you all the recipes. Full disclosure: I've stolen most of them. I enjoy cooking, but I'm no Alice Waters. My real talent is hosting." She swiped a layer of flour dust off the counter with her finger. Letting go of some responsibilities was a relief in some ways—but bitter in others.

Emma sat in the truck, fingers tapping on the steering wheel as she waited for Henry to exit at the same time he did every afternoon for his lunch break.

"Maybe he's off investigating," Tim said, leaning against the passenger window.

Emma scoffed. "I'm the only one who does any investigating around here."

She spotted Henry striding down the curved sidewalk toward his car. She jumped out, leaving the engine running.

"Henry!" She waved at him as she rushed over.

"Emma." He sounded unimpressed with her unannounced arrival. "If you're here about your car, you're out of luck. My team is still searching for clues." He retrieved a small notebook from his back pocket. "Do you have any enemies I could interview?"

"Well, I did accuse Kevin days before."

Henry sighed, his fingers pushing up his oval-rimmed glasses. He didn't seem to buy it for one second—obviously still in denial that a murderer could be lurking through the streets, despite all the evidence to the contrary. Nonetheless, he wrote Kevin's name down on the page.

"That's not why I'm here, though," Emma said. "I wanted to know if you got to that USB I sent in."

"It's with the forensic team now to verify its authenticity. Still, we may be out of luck in using it to convict anybody because, according to wiretapping laws, at least one person in the conversation must consent. Seeing as Alexander is dead, that would leave Monroe, who I doubt would want this evidence hanging over his head."

"But it at least gives you a reason to investigate him and Kevin for the murder, right? They both had motives."

"Having motive doesn't make someone a murderer. Search hard enough, and you could find motive in almost anyone who knew him—even Amber."

"Amber?"

Henry shrugged. "I'm surprised you haven't considered her. Spouses are always the first to be considered in homicides. But I suppose knowing the suspects creates bias. Another reason you should leave it to the proper authorities."

His words felt like a slap in the face. Of course, she hadn't suspected Amber—because she *knew* Amber; she had known her since grade school. Amber couldn't even squash a bug let alone shoot her own husband in the head.

No, it couldn't be her. It just couldn't.

Emma was washing some dirty dishes when she spotted streaks of flashing light outside the window. She flipped on the porch lights, which revealed Julia Hedwink with a flashlight and binoculars, looking up toward Chad Monroe's bedroom.

"What are you doing, Julia?" Emma asked through the crack of the window.

No wonder Monroe called her unhinged.

"The same as you," Julia answered.

Emma let her curiosity get the better of her and unlatched the back door. "I don't think you'll catch many clues looking through windows. Trust me, I've tried that before," she said, thinking back to Kevin's hotel room. "Come on in for a cup of tea, if you want."

Julia lowered the binoculars and walked through the door. The whiff of her synthetic rose perfume burned Emma's nostrils.

Emma went over to set the kettle on the burner.

"What would you like?" she asked, grabbing an assortment of tea boxes.

"Chamomile would be great." Julia sat on the same stool Amber always claimed.

Emma missed her friend's visits and wondered how long it would take till she felt healed enough to be able to come back.

"That's a good one before bed." Emma set the mug with the tea bag in front of her.

"So." Emma sat across from her. "Why do you think Monroe killed Alexander?"

Julia lifted one perfectly sculpted eyebrow. "I know they found a gun with a navy insignia beside the body, and I know Monroe was after something from him. That recent almost-break-in at the Kirks'—that was Monroe. I followed him to the end of the driveway. When I saw the alarm go off, I left ASAP, of course, before he could spot me."

"You're certain it was him?" Emma had only caught a glimpse of the shadowed figure, but what she did catch didn't have Chad's big build.

"Yeah. Like I said, I was following his car. My room is just beside his and I heard when he got up. The walls here are paper thin and his alarm is super loud." She cringed.

"It's an old building," Emma said. "Just wood and wallpaper."

The whistle on the kettle blew, spitting fragments of steam into the air. Emma fetched it and poured the hot liquid into Julia's cup. "What else do you know?"

"I don't know much, but I suspect plenty."

"Okay, and what do you suspect?"

"Amber was in on it." Julia stirred her tea with the tea bag instead of the spoon Emma had set on the small plate. Her eyes were downcast, so she didn't catch Emma's exasperated expression.

"You're wrong. I've known Amber forever. She is certainly no killer."

"I didn't say she was a killer, but she would've known her husband's route perfectly, right? Every stop, every turn."

"I'm not so sure. She rarely went with him. It was too early for her."

"Well, someone would have had to have leaked that route to Monroe, and I think she would've been that someone. I saw Chad and Amber together at Redmond's Bar just a week ago. They looked like they were discussing something important. I couldn't hear a word, unfortunately, since I was watching from the parking lot."

"Well, Monroe and Alexander could've arranged to meet up. Or Kevin…"

"Maybe, but my gut's telling me Amber was in on it, and my gut's never wrong. You'd feel the same way if you weren't so biased. Chloe sees it too—I can tell."

"Why do you say that?"

"I saw her watching them at the bar. The way she looked at Amber—it was obvious. I recognized that look. She suspects her, mark my words."

Emma's hand shook as she poured herself a cup of tea, causing the boiling water to splash her counter. The image of Amber holding a shaking gun to her husband's head, asking if he was having an affair, flashed through Emma's mind. No. No. That wasn't Amber. She was sassy and strong-willed, but when sadness hit, she was the type to fold into a fetal position and lie in the shower with clothes still on, sobbing. Emma knew this because she had seen it when Amber's mother died.

And if Amber had found out about her husband having an affair, wouldn't Emma have been the first person she would have turned to? They had been best friends since grade school. They always told each other everything.

"I didn't mean to upset you," Julia said, looking up at her through her double-layered fake eyelashes.

"I'm not upset," Emma responded quickly. "I was just thinking. Sorry."

"Maybe we could work together," Julia said coolly, taking another sip of her tea. "I want to find out who killed Alexander just as much as you do, believe me. Alexander was more than just my boss. He was my friend. We spent a lot of after-office hours at the bar together. I learned a lot about him from those talks—how noble he was, how devoted to his marriage and family, and how impossible it would be for him to take his own life."

"I appreciate the sentiment, but I prefer to work alone."

"I get it. You and your granddaughter acting as detectives together must be a novelty."

"That's not what's going on."

"Don't worry." Julia laughed. "Your secret is safe with me." She picked up her mug. "Can I bring it back to my room?"

"Sure."

"And thanks for the chat. I'm glad I'm not the only crazy one trying to find Alex's killer." She winked before heading out the swaying doors.

Chapter Twenty-Eight

It was only six a.m., so Ash hadn't arrived yet. Chloe and Granny Em sat alone in the kitchen, sipping hot coffee and munching on day-old bacon from yesterday's breakfast.

"Is Amber on your list of suspects?" Granny Em asked.

"Uh…" Chloe wiped her greasy fingers on her apron. Had Granny Em meant for her tone to sound accusatory, or was Chloe just imagining it? Either way, she knew this would be a sore subject.

"Just be honest."

Chloe held back the words that were on the tip of her tongue. "I mean, yeah, low on the list, but she was his wife and knew he was having an affair—-so there was motive." Chloe cleared her throat. "Like, do I think she's capable of that? I don't know. You don't seem to, and you know her better than me, so…"

"What do you mean, she knew?"

"Jared told me," Chloe said. "He said that's why it couldn't be her—because she already knew about the affair and still held on to hope, waiting for Alexander to come to his senses. But Jared also said he heard her leave after Alexander that morning, so I was thinking—just as a weak possibility—that maybe she followed him, killed him in a heat of rage, then came home, cleaned up, and called you in distress. And because she was so distressed, she might've let it slip that he was dead—without explaining how she knew that." Chloe shrugged. "It's just a theory. But I don't know her all that well, and I trust your judgment."

Granny Em nodded. "Well, I appreciate that. I don't think it could've been her. She can't even stand killing flies, and I'm not sure she knows how to fire a gun."

"You're probably right. Plus, super dark if she was the one that targeted you. Like, you're her best friend! So, yeah, my bet's on Kevin or Chad."

"Mine too," Granny Em said softly, stirring a spoonful of sugar into her coffee, which Chloe noted was very unlike her. She never took sugar in her coffee.

Just as Chloe was about to say more, Ash came in through the back door, red hair bobbing up and down against her shoulders.

"Hey, Chloe!"

"Hey." Chloe gave a small wave. She liked Ash—she was nice and the closest person to her age here. Maybe, in time, they could even be friends.

"Okay, what's on the list today, Boss?" Ash asked Granny Em after she had hung up her backpack and tied her apron.

"Just bacon, scrambled eggs, and fruit salad," Granny Em said. "You can get to work on the salad. I'll get the bacon going."

Chloe peeked out the doors to see Julia and Susan already at table nine. "Table nine is waiting," she said. "I'll bring them some coffee."

She didn't wait for Granny Em to acknowledge her, she just left with the piping hot coffee and a saucer of cream.

"My mom's losing her mind," Chloe heard Susan say. "She thinks I'm psycho or something and said she'd call the cops on me—all because of my art!"

Julia laughed wildly. "Why'd you let her see it?"

"I didn't. She broke into my home; said it was the same thing as her going in to clean my room when I lived with her. She even took a lot of it to burn in her fireplace. She's a crazy bat!"

"Sounds like a narc."

"Good morning!" Chloe interrupted, with the usual fake chirpy voice that she felt suited her role as waitress here. "Today we just have eggs, bacon, fruit salad, or toast."

"No vegan options?" Susan asked.

Since when was she a vegan? She had ordered bacon just last week. "Uh, I could ask."

Susan waved her hand. "It's fine, just bring me some toast and fruit salad."

"I'll have eggs, bacon, and fruit salad," Julia said.

Chloe wrote up their orders in her pocket-sized notebook. "Okay. Great. Coffee?" She asked, lifting the pot.

"Sure." Julia pushed her cup toward Chloe who poured the hot liquid into it, filling the area with the nutty scent.

"Just water for me," Susan said. "New diet."

Julia laughed, looking her friend over. "As if you need it. You're a twig!"

"I need to detox."

"Yeah, okay. Try not to faint, then."

Chloe headed back to the kitchen to fetch some water for the now-vegan Susan.

She slid the note across the counter to Ash. "First order of the day," she said.

"Where's Susan's mom live?" She whispered to Granny Em who was by the sink.

"Just down Elm Street. Number 224. Why?"

"Oh, just wondering. She said her mother wanted to call the cops on her because of some art she painted."

"Anne *is* a little batty," Granny Em said. "And they've always been at odds. I don't think the answers lie in her art."

"Maybe not, but worth checking out. Maybe her mother will show us what she confiscated."

"Well, Tim and I will have to tag along if you go. With what happened to my car, we can't take any chances. Not that I think Anne's a killer. She's crazy, but not a killer."

"Yeah, okay, fine. After breakfast, then?"

"Sure. I'll bring my muffins. That'll get us through the door without a hitch."

Chloe's pops chose to wait outside in the truck. He was not too keen on talking with Anne and clearly didn't think the girls were too much at risk.

"Don't take long," he said. "I was just in the middle of patching the fence out back. I need to get back to it before the sun sets."

"You think we'll be in there that long?" Granny Em laughed. "I'd die!"

She grabbed the muffins from the backseat and followed Chloe to the front door. The neighborhood was quaint but a little rundown with old wood houses one after the other, all painted white or a soft yellow. Anne's was the most rundown of all with a splintered porch and rickety steps that had holes in them.

"Man, her yard is depressing," Chloe said, looking around at the overgrown grass and vines of poison ivy wrapping around her broken fence.

"Yeah, her husband died from cancer a few years ago. He was the one that tended the yard."

"That's sad."

Chloe knocked on the door.

"Coming!" A voice called out. "But bringing my baseball bat in case you're a solicitor, so better run if you are!"

Chloe made a face. "She sounds pleasant."

"Don't say I didn't warn you."

Several locks could be heard unfastening before the door swung open, revealing Anne hunched over a walker. She was a lot older than Chloe was expecting given Susan's age. She must've had her in her forties.

"What are you two doing on my doorstep?" Anne wrinkled her nose at them.

"You've probably heard, I'm investigating Alexander's death." Granny Em held up the plate of muffins.

Anne stepped aside. "I'd normally shut the door in your faces. I loathe interviews but can't say no to your muffins, so come on in."

The dingy place smelled like cat urine. Chloe tried not to gag.

Anne led them to a small living area where two arm chairs and a couch faced an unlit fireplace. Chloe slowed her pace as she passed the newspapers and logs set out for kindling. Sure enough, just as Susan claimed, her artwork was among them.

Chloe restrained a gasp when she saw the paintings. One was of Julia and Alexander sitting by the beach under an umbrella as rain drizzled down. Julia was huddled up close to him, her red trench coat wrapped around her. Another showed the two of them sharing a kiss in an alleyway. The last was of Alexander lying dead, red lipstick smeared on his cheek.

Were these events Susan had witnessed? Did she know who the killer was? The crime scene wasn't identical to what Chloe saw in the video, but it was too close for comfort and it made Chloe wonder how Susan could possibly know all these details.

"I mean to burn those," Anne said, startling Chloe. "My daughter likes to draw stories, you see. Whatever snippets of gossip she hears fuels her passion." Anne laughed, settling into one of the armchairs. "I like gossip too, don't get me wrong, but to paint it? That just looks bad."

"Were these things she saw?" Chloe asked, approaching the couch. She was hesitant to sit on it, given the smell of the place, and certainly didn't want to bring home fleas or smell like cat feces. She did eventually sit down, though, inwardly cringing as her body made impact with the cushion.

"I doubt it. She's just imaginative and maybe a tinge mentally ill—like her father."

"How so?"

"She gets strange ideas into her head sometimes. It's why she's thirty and unmarried still. She has sabotaged every single relationship under the sun, mine included. Won't even talk to me—thinks I'm controlling and possessive. But she's the possessive one!"

"She's managed to keep one friend at least," Chloe said, lowering her hand on the arm rest and then pulling it quickly back into her lap once she noticed the thick layer of loose cat fur.

"Julia has no idea." Anne laughed. "No idea. Won't be long before Susan turns on her just like she has me."

Granny Em, who was sitting in the other arm-chair, leant forward, eyeing the papers. "I had no idea Susan even drew. Did you teach her?"

"Oh no. Don't know where she learned. I certainly didn't teach her or pay for any classes. She is good at it, I'll admit that much. Maybe if she drew flowers or something, she could sell them, but like I said, it's all just random events from town and not joyful ones, either. You remember that hit-and-run five years ago? She painted a whole mural in her hallway based on that. Twisted if you ask me."

"Do you think these were things she witnessed?" Granny Em asked.

Anne shook her head. "Not unless she has eyes all over town." She reached for a muffin and took a bite. "You can come over anytime for a gossip if you bring me these," she said with her mouth full.

Granny Em smiled. "I'm glad you like them."

"So." Anne pointed a crumb-coated finger at Emma. "You're a sleuth now, playing copper." She laughed. "I remember my daughter telling me how you solved all these petty mysteries back in high school, but you're grown up now, right?" She laughed again.

Chloe was beginning to see why her grandmother disliked her.

"I wouldn't say I'm playing at anything." Granny Em cleared her throat. "I'm just trying to figure out the truth. I don't think Alexander killed himself." Her grandmother looked toward the piles of artwork. "Clearly, your daughter doesn't think so either."

"Like I said, she's crazy. Now." Anne took another muffin from the plate. "What did you come to talk about?"

"We just wanted to know if you knew anything. I mean, they say you have ears everywhere."

"Yeah, I do." She flashed a sly smile. "It's what boredom does to you."

"So, what have you heard?"

"Well, he was obviously having an affair going on for at least two years. Susan knew this. She drew it all over her wall. Good thing Julia never visits her at her place. She'd be perturbed, I think."

"I'm surprised *you* kept quiet," Granny Em said.

Anne shrugged. "I have some wit about me. I know that when the person I'm about to gossip about has a handful of lawyers, I should mince my words. It was hard, though, trying to keep that secret." She let out a heavy sigh. "Least he's dead now. I don't need to worry as much about keeping his hidden life a secret anymore."

"What else about him have you been keeping hidden?"

"Mostly that, but I've heard some things around the block—like that the butler had him under his boot all because he saved him once. He'd demand money; even demanded Alexander change his will."

"Who told you this?" Granny Em asked.

"I don't give away my sources, sorry."

Chloe bit her cheek. "That doesn't sound like Jared. He seems pretty down-to-earth to me. I mean, I get it's weird Alexander left him the house, but Jared *did* save his life."

Anne shrugged. "I don't judge. I just report." Then she laughed. "Actually, scratch that—I do judge, a lot. I never liked the mousy butler. If anyone killed Alex, it was probably him, but I'm not about to step on Henry's toes. Not my place, not yours neither. Let the rich man's bones lie."

Granny Em looked down at her wristwatch and then out the window. "We better go. Thanks for the chat, Anne. Maybe we'll stop by another time."

Chloe jumped up a bit too eagerly. As much as she found this conversation enlightening, she was itching to get out of this place. First thing she was going to do was get back and hop in the shower.

"Did you get a good look at those paintings?" Chloe asked once they were on the doorstep.

"I did. It was very eerie how many details she got correct. Do you think she saw the murder?"

"No idea, but at least I know why I get the jeebies when I'm around her. She's super weird."

Pops rolled down the window as they crossed the street. "Look at that sun." He pointed to the sun sinking down. "Thought you said you'd only be half an hour."

"Yeah, I know, sorry." Her grandmother slid into the passenger seat.

Pops plugged his nose. "Oh man, you reek."

Chloe sniffed her shirt and shivered. "Yeah, get us home quick. I'm about ready to barf after being in there."

Pops laughed. "Yeah, you don't have to tell me twice. Windows stay down. All of them."

Susan stood on the porch, her dark hair pulled back under a head wrap, purse slung over her shoulder.

Emma watched as her eyes darted—old ladies, the garden, the parking lot, the lake—never settling.

Emma pushed back from the front desk and opened the door. "Waiting for Julia?"

Susan stepped closer. "Yeah."

Emma joined her on the porch, arms crossed. "I visited your mother the other day."

Susan stiffened. Her lips parted, like she wanted to gasp but wouldn't let herself. "Why would you do that?"

"I'm interviewing people about what happened," Emma said. "And I saw your artwork." She studied Susan's reaction. "You drew some very detailed pictures of the crime scene. Did you see it happen?" She paused. "Tell me about the red lipstick."

"It was just symbolic. Maybe his wife kissed him the night before. I made a story up in my head, is all."

"I would normally believe you, except I saw him on the scene and what you drew—it matched. Did you see it happen, Susan? Do you know who killed him?"

"I mean yeah, probably, it is a small town," she said with a smirk.

"Stop playing around."

Susan sucked in a shaky breath and whispered, "I was the one who found him, okay? I called it in, but I didn't do it. I wouldn't. I'm not a murderer."

"What were you doing on the beach that early?"

"Walking Gretel. She gets antsy around screaming kids, so in the summer, I take her out before the crowds."

"So, you found him?"

"Well, more like Gretel found him. I probably wouldn't have noticed if she hadn't started barking like a maniac and trying to escape to get to him."

"Did you hear the gunshot?"

"I did, and it startled me, but I don't know. I didn't think much of it. I just thought it was the construction on Turk Street."

"What time would you say?"

"Half-past five. I know 'cause I happened to look at my clock just before. Julia and I were supposed to meet up for breakfast, and I wanted to get back in time to change."

Emma made a mental note. Half-past five. Amber called her at 5:50.

"So, what did you see? Did you see the suspect?"

"No. I wasn't nearby when the shot was fired, and it wasn't till I got closer that Gretel went berserk."

"Did you see any footprints?"

"I don't know. All I could see was the body, and all I could do was keep Gretel away from it. Everything else is a blur. I was in shock, you know."

"So, why paint it?"

"To process it. Usually when I paint the things that worry me, it stops those obsessive thoughts."

Emma let that sit for a beat. Then, "But you painted Julia's affair. Why? Were you worried about that, too?"

Susan swallowed hard, her fingers twitching. "I was conflicted." Her gaze locked onto the doorway. "I didn't agree with it. Kevin was a good guy, and I felt like she was throwing away something solid.

But... I didn't say anything. I have a hard time keeping friends. If I called her out, she might've cut me off."

The door handle turned. Susan's lips pressed into a tight line, but the moment she saw Julia, she forced a smile. She turned and shot Emma a glare.

Emma held back a smirk. "Thanks, Susan," she said. "Tell your mom I enjoyed our visit."

Chapter Twenty-Nine

The scent of synthetic rose perfume was the first thing to greet Emma as she walked into the kitchen. On top of the box of cookies she planned to set out at the front desk as yummy freebies were a note and a necklace coated in sand.

Found this on the beach right where Alexander died. Recognize it? - Julia

Emma picked it up. She did recognize it, her mind flashing back to Amber sitting at the counter, chewing this very necklace. Had she dropped it when viewing the dead body? That made no sense unless she had it in her pocket, but why would she? It wasn't like it was a phone.

Emma turned it over and noticed the clasp was broken. Had Alexander yanked it from her neck? Had she killed him in self-defence?

Her head spun. She rubbed at her temples and plopped down on the closest stool. *This makes no sense. Amber can't be the killer.* And yet…

Emma sucked in a shaky breath and stuffed the necklace into her apron pocket just as Ash came waltzing in, cheery as usual.

"Hello, Boss." She bobbed her head. "What's on the menu for today?"

Emma grabbed the recipe cards she had printed out just for Ash and set them on the counter. "I already made the French toast casserole. It just needs to be warmed up. So, I'd say start with the bacon and eggs. Julia prefers poached with hollandaise sauce. I've run out of hollandaise, so you'll have to make it from scratch." Emma held up one of the cards that was coloured pink. "You gotta add the melted butter slowly because you don't want to risk scrambling the eggs. Ask me how I know." She winked, setting the card in front of Ash.

Ash pinned her frizzy curls back with some bobby pins and put the mesh covering over her sweaty head. "All right. I think I can manage."

"You busy?" Tim asked.

"Why?" Emma asked, sauntering over and linking arms with her husband.

"I was in the mood for a stroll and was wondering if you wanted to join me."

"Ash might need me present."

"I'm good," Ash interjected. "You left me alone like my first day of work and I still survived. I'm sure I can manage a week in. I got my cards and Chloe will be down to help me serve the guests, right?"

"Yeah, I'll go get her," Emma said. "All right." She kissed Tim's cheek. "I'll meet you out front."

Tim and Emma walked across the crooked sidewalks. Crow's high school stood at the far end of the street.

"We should check it out," Emma said. "It's been a long time since I've entered those grounds."

"Yeah, okay." Tim held her hand as they walked toward it, keeping his body on the side of the walkway that faced the road.

As Emma approached the brick walls, she could almost picture Alexander sitting on top, feet dangling over. They were always sitting up there together, much to the principal's disapproval. It was dangerous being so high up, but they would use Alexander's trunk to hoist themselves up there.

"They were so in love," Emma whispered, remembering it all. "Just as in love as we were."

Tim nudged her. "I doubt that."

"Yet, he betrayed her, essentially left her for another woman. Why? How? Is that just what men do when a prettier, younger woman starts to show interest?"

"I've had plenty of young women come on to me, but I'm still here with my one and only," Tim said, wrapping his arm around Emma. "So, no, don't think so. That's what a weak character does, not a man who knows what he signed up for when he made his vows."

He was right. He'd had plenty of women chase him even after marriage. It was almost a weekly occurrence even in this small town, especially during summer with so many tourists. Yet, Tim always dismissed the advances.

"I just can't get over it." Emma looked into Tim's chestnut eyes. "I know you're loyal to me, but I just can't help but wonder how our fates looked so similar, and now…I don't know. I just feel unworthy of my good fortune—of you. And insecure and…"

"Stop it." He tightened his grip on her. "They've always been different from us. Alexander was my buddy, but besides football, we didn't have much in common. I feel like all these years, it's been this history here that's kept all of us so close," he said, pointing at the school building. "But in reality, I think we're very different people and you and I are certainly not bound to repeat their mistakes. I certainly won't ever cheat on you, if that's what you're so worried about. I love you, desperately. Always have, always will. Even when your looks fade and you become some wrinkled old hag." He laughed as he caught a smile on her lips. "Even then, I'd still choose you over the prettiest woman in the world."

"You sure do know how to melt a girl's heart," she said, leaning in to kiss him.

Emma stepped into Amber's house, instantly uneasy. The air was thick, the dim hallway flickering with unsteady light. The silence between the hum of the bulbs felt unnatural.

"Amber?" she called, her voice barely above a whisper. She moved forward slowly, each step creaking against the hardwood. "Hello?"

A sound—muffled but unmistakable—drifted toward her. Voices. Raised. Angry. Coming from Alexander's office.

"I saw you kissing her! You can't hide it anymore!" Amber's voice cracked with fury; her words soaked in betrayal.

Emma froze.

"Just calm down," Alexander said, his tone low, placating. Emma could almost see his hands lifted, trying to steady the storm.

"You're going to leave me, aren't you?" Amber choked out.

"Amber, we haven't been happy for a while. It's time. You know it's time." A pause. Keys hitting the wood desk. "You can have the house. I wouldn't leave you with nothing."

Emma edged forward, her pulse hammering.

"After everything? High school, boot camp, the moves, the years of waiting for you—and now you throw it all away for someone as young as your daughter?"

"I care about you, Amber. I want you to be happy."

Emma's pace quickened, but the hallway seemed to stretch endlessly. A trick of the mind, panic twisting time.

Then—

Bang*.*

The shot tore through the air. Deafening.

Emma stumbled, ears ringing, hands instinctively covering them. Silence swallowed the house. No more arguing. No more voices.

Just quiet.

"Amber!" she shouted, sprinting the last few steps. The office door loomed ahead—closed, locked. She fumbled

with the knob and pressed against it, her pulse throbbing, throat constricting.

From the other side, muffled sobs.

Emma's fingers tightened around the doorknob. "Amber, open the door! Amber!"

But all she could hear was her friend's voice through the wood: "What have I done? Oh, Alex…"

Emma bolted up in bed, heart pounding heavy against her chest. Moonlight stretched through the window and kissed her toes that stuck out from under the blanket.

Tim rolled over and looked up at her. "What is it?" he asked in a drowsy voice, his eyes hardly open.

"I can't keep doing this." Tears sprung to Emma's eyes. She pulled the blanket tight around her trembling frame. "I don't want to find out."

Tim sat up and brought her close to his chest. "What are you going on about? Find out what?" He rubbed her back.

"The killer. I don't want to find the killer…not anymore."

"Because you're scared?"

"Yes, but not for myself. I'm scared of who it is—that it's Amber."

Tim suppressed a chuckle. "You clearly are delirious right now and need to go back to bed. You and I both know it can't be Amber."

"But why couldn't it?" Emma looked up at him, trying to steady herself by looking into his brown eyes. "Alexander was having an affair—that gives her motive. Somehow, she knew he was dead—how?"

"Amber jumps to the worst-case scenarios all the time. That's nothing new. And you really think she tampered with your car? I doubt she even knows how to change a wheel! Seriously, Ems, you're worrying over nothing." He kissed the top of her head. "Just take some breaths. You have known Amber your whole life. If she was capable of this, you'd be the first to see it."

"But what if I don't *know* her? Jared said she knew Alexander was having an affair, but she never told me. I would've expected her to tell me. There's always been an understanding that we tell each other everything. Why wouldn't she have told me?"

"Maybe it was to protect him. Maybe she was worried that if you knew it would change the whole dynamic of our friend group, I don't know. She could've even been ashamed or in denial. Plenty of reasons why she'd keep it a secret. And who knows? Maybe Jared's wrong. Maybe there was never even an affair to begin with."

"I don't think he was wrong, but you could be right. She's a proud creature. It could've been some sense of shame holding her back."

"See." Tim brushed his lips across her cheek. "Come on. Lie down."

Emma sank back down into her pillows. She closed her eyes and tried to sleep, but her mind was on fire. *What if Tim's wrong? No, he's right. Even if she killed Alex in a fury of passion, she'd never deliberately hurt me. Would she? No. This is Amber. She isn't capable of killing. She's my friend. I know her.*

Silvia sat across from Emma, sipping cherry pop while Emma cradled a steaming cup of tea. Fizzy drinks always made Emma sneeze, so she avoided them.

"Well, your bed-and-breakfast is finally running like a dream," Silvia said, leaning back to take it all in. "I can go home knowing I've made a difference."

Emma followed her gaze to the beautifully tended garden. Not long ago, it had been a mess—wild weeds tangled with tomato vines, choking the life out of the plants. Now, everything was neatly sectioned, the weeds were gone, and the flowers bloomed in perfect harmony. Inside, Ash had fully taken over the kitchen, and the new secretary was bubbly, likable, and nearly as intuitive as Emma when it came to anticipating guests' needs.

"I know. I almost feel useless now," Emma said with a grin. "Thank you, Silvia. I should've done this a long time ago." *Back when Bella was still a baby.*

Silvia smirked. "I bet it feels good to actually relax—and go on a few date nights again."

"Oh, absolutely. Tim definitely owes you. He's been much happier since the changes." Emma grabbed a cookie and took a bite. "I'll miss you, though. Are you sure you can't stay a little longer?"

Silvia sighed. "William's already getting antsy. Ever since the kids moved out, he gets lonely when I'm gone too long."

"He can't fly down for a few days?"

She shook her head. "Work's keeping him busy, and you know how much he hates the humidity here." She shrugged. "It's okay. Honestly, I'm starting to miss my own bed. Nothing like home."

"No, there isn't," Emma agreed, smiling.

Chapter Thirty

The morning rush had slowed, and Ash was untying her apron and hanging it up by the front door.

"I'm going to go hang out on the docks," she said. "See you for lunch."

Emma nodded. "See you."

Emma plopped down on a stool, inhaling the leftover smell of toast and bacon. Her phone vibrated, and she took it out of her pocket to see a text from Amber.

'Want to come by this afternoon? Jared has some type of appointment that he's being all weird about for some reason, so it'll just be me in this empty house till noon, and I'll be honest, I don't like being alone.'

Emma typed back: *'Yeah, you can count on me. Make the tea and I'll bring some biscuits and cream.'*

Emma thought, *I wonder if his appointment concerns the USB. Maybe the police called him in for questioning since he found it. That would explain why he's being weird about it.*

Emma set the phone down and walked over to the pantry. She only had a couple of hours to whip up some delicious homemade biscuits.

She crouched down and pulled out the heavy bag of flour. She didn't bother carrying it over to the counter. Not worth the strain. Instead, she just grabbed a handheld measuring cup and scooped what she needed into a glass bowl, which she then carried over to the counter.

After she was done and her whole kitchen smelled like fresh bread—the best scent ever, she set the biscuits on a cooling rack.

"Those for me?" Tim asked, reaching for one.

Emma playfully smacked his hand away. "They're for Amber, but if there are leftovers, you can try one then."

"No way you and Amber would eat over a dozen biscuits."

Emma laughed. "Some are for the guests. It'll save Ash cooking time."

Emma began placing jam, butter, and fresh cream in small airtight containers. Then she took seven still-hot biscuits, blew on them, and placed them on a plate. "All right, gotta go. Let Ash know the rest are for the guests."

"Wait." Tim held up a finger. "I thought we had a deal. I go with you everywhere."

Emma groaned. "I really need some girl time, though."

"I'll stay in the truck. I promise."

"You'd stay in the truck the whole time?" She laughed.

"It's not such a hard sacrifice. I'll bring a book."

Emma kissed his cheek. "Okay, Mr. Knight-In-Shining-Armor. Go grab that book."

Emma parked the truck near the rushing waterfall at the cul-de-sac of the lot. "I'll try not to be too long," she said, kissing her husband's lips. "Keep your sword ready, just in case." She looked out the window. "You never know what strange cars might drive on up."

"I'll keep my eyes peeled." He winked. "Have fun with your friend and save me a biscuit!"

Emma knocked on Amber's front door, her gaze drifting to the towering pillars and the intricate engraving of two horses racing along the stone frame. A moment later, the door creaked open.

Amber stood there, eyes shadowed with exhaustion. "Thanks for coming." She stepped aside, gesturing Emma in. "If you don't mind, let's go to the library. The rest of the house…" She swallowed, rubbing her arms. "I can't handle it today. Grief's weird that way."

Emma nodded. "Yeah, sure, that's fine."

Emma walked down the long hallway, wincing as she passed Alexander's office, remembering her dream.

The library had more than just books scattered about it. Amber had made it into a makeshift bedroom. A mattress was laid out across the floor, sheets and blankets crumpled at the end of it. A mess of plates full of unfinished meals cluttered the mahogany table beside it.

Amber dropped into a chair, pushing a cup of tea toward Emma. "So…have you recovered from your car trying to kill you?"

Emma blinked. "I didn't realize you heard about that."

"Jared told me." She took a bite of a biscuit, letting the crumbs fall onto her lap. "I'm glad you're okay."

"Yeah, your hill saved me." Emma took a sip of tea. It was a little bitter—likely over-steeped. "The mechanic claims it was sabotage."

Amber's jaw fell. "You're kidding?"

"No."

Amber trembled and rubbed her head. "You really think there's a murderer in our midst? You think he's after you now?"

"I'm not sure. Maybe."

A shaky breath left Amber's lips, and a tear slid down her cheek. "Everyone I love…why?" It was said so softly, Emma hardly caught it.

Relief filled Emma. Surely Amber couldn't have done it—not with a response like that. "I'll be fine. Tim's been keeping close tabs on me ever since. Even if it's Monroe, Tim would be a worthy match."

"You think it's Monroe?" Her eyes widened.

"I don't know. Maybe. You don't?"

Amber shook her head. "I don't know. No one seems likely in my mind."

"That's all right. Don't worry about it."

Amber looked down at the half-eaten biscuit in her hand, turning it over between her fingers. "Thanks for the offering," she said. "I'm still utterly broken, but I'm at least able to eat again."

Emma studied her friend. Once chubby, Amber now looked almost as thin as she'd been in high school. "I'm glad," she said softly, glancing around. "Is this your new bedroom?"

Amber sighed. "It's a disaster, I know."

"We could make it into something special." Emma nudged her shoulder. "Want some help?"

Amber swayed slightly, considering, then nodded. "All right. Let's do it."

They set to work. Emma pulled the curtains apart, letting the golden light flood the room. Outside, evergreens brushed against the windowpanes, their dark branches framing the glimmering blue waters beyond.

Amber remade her bed properly, then started clearing out the mess, tossing old food into the trash. She moved slowly, taking frequent breaks—grief weighing on her like chains.

"Do you have any fairy lights?" Emma asked.

"In the basement, with the Christmas decorations."

"Be right back."

Emma descended the basement steps, suppressing a shudder. The place was always a disaster—dust-covered boxes stacked haphazardly, cobwebs clinging to the corners. The Kirks really needed to hire someone to organize it. It took nearly half an hour to find the lights, and another ten minutes to untangle them. She grabbed a few fake flowers as well. *Hopefully Tim isn't too bored,* she thought to herself as she dragged what she found up the old rickety steps.

Amber was still smoothing out the sheets when Emma returned.

Setting to work, Emma draped the lights across the bookshelves, weaving the delicate flowers between the green wires. When she stepped back, she nodded in approval. "That'll do for now. Tim's waiting for me in the car, so I should probably go."

"What?" Amber nearly gasped.

"Yeah, he won't let me out of his sight since the incident." Emma walked over to Amber, who was sitting on her newly made bed. "But hey, we made tremendous progress already. Now it looks more like a proper place to call *your* room."

"It does. Thank you." Amber stood and interweaved her fingers with Emma's. "You're a good friend."

Chapter Thirty-One

Chloe sat on the windowsill of her bedroom, looking through the window with her binoculars. A blue jay sat in the branches of a cypress tree, head burrowed into its chest, but she wasn't birdwatching. She was people-watching.

Her gaze flicked to Susan and Julia, sitting in Susan's car with the windows down. Susan cradled a paper cup of coffee, laughing at something. Julia, however, wasn't laughing back. She looked distracted. Chloe followed her line of sight—straight to Chad Monroe.

Emma had told Chloe about the note Monroe claimed Julia had left him. Was he the killer and was Julia his next target?

Ring. Ring.

Chloe let the binoculars fall to her chest and grabbed her phone.

"Hello?"

"Hey, Detective," Mike said. "I looked into Kevin like you asked. Couldn't find much, but his wife, Julia, has got a history of erratic behavior. My cousin's in the police force—I had him run her name along with the others. She's been arrested multiple times for disturbing the peace, even violence against an ex. No charges were pressed, though. Maybe the guy was embarrassed."

Chloe's grip tightened on the phone. That lipstick stain on Alexander's cheek flickered in her mind. Had Julia and Alexander shared one last fling before his walk? If so, why hadn't he wiped it off?

But then, if Julia did kill him, why leave blatant evidence of the fact on his cheek? That was the mark of a serial killer, and Chloe didn't think that's who they were dealing with. So, it was either a blunder or a deliberate attempt of the real killer to point the finger at her.

She lifted the binoculars back up and zeroed in on the auburn-haired beauty, whose eyes were still glued on Monroe.

"And the others?" she asked.

"All clean, besides the occasional speeding ticket. No violent crimes."

"Even Jared?"

"Yeah. Totally clean."

Chloe exhaled, her breath fogging the glass, blurring her vision of the two women.

"Thanks for the help, Mike."

Chloe slid off the windowsill and made her way to the kitchen, where she knew she'd find her grandmother.

As she pushed open the doors, the rich scent of butter and cinnamon wrapped around her.

"Grab an apron if you want to help," Granny Em said over the steady whir of the mixer. "I'm working on my famous muffins."

Chloe pulled an apron over her head, tucking her hair under a plastic covering.

"What's your secret?" Chloe asked, peering over her shoulder.

Granny Em winked. "Extra butter." She shut off the mixer and began scooping batter into the muffin tin. "What's on your mind?"

Chloe picked up a spoon to help. "I just talked to Mike. He found out Julia was arrested once for attacking an ex. No charges were filed, though."

Granny Em arched her brow. "Could've been self-defence."

"Maybe, but wouldn't she have been the one to call the cops if it was?"

Granny Em shrugged. "You'd be surprised how manipulative some people can be."

The oven beeped.

"Just in time," her grandmother said, opening the door. A blast of warm air rushed out, curling around them.

Chloe hesitated, then asked, "So you don't think it's her?"

Granny Em slid the tray inside. "I can't quite picture someone as dainty as her crawling under my car, but I haven't ruled her out. Still, she's been sending me clues to help. Why would she do that if she were the killer?"

Chloe bit her lip. "Yeah… I guess."

Chapter Thirty-Two

Chloe walked along the shore, stepping into the footprints left by others—some belonging to small children, others to grown men. She thought of their stories. Did that child have a past like hers—invisible, just someone there to feed and shelter, but hardly interact with? Or were they seen, held tight to the chest of their mother?

Her phone rang, and she took it out of her pocket. She answered it instinctively, thinking it was Emma calling to check up on her. She wasn't supposed to be out on her own.

"Hello?"

"Hey, Chloe." It was her mom. "Just calling to check in. I don't have much time."

Chloe rolled her eyes. Of course not. This was just what her mother did so she could convince herself she was not being neglectful.

"It's okay, Mom. You can spare yourself the trouble. I'm fine."

"I'm glad to hear it. I just wanted to talk about when you get home—because it'll be soon, ya know. Summer is coming to an end—and I just want to talk about some expectations for when you get back."

Chloe sighed. She did not want to hear about any expectations.

"I know I forgot your birthday, but you did majorly overreact, and I just want to set us both up for success when you return. I need you to understand that I work hard for you so I can give you a great life with so many opportunities. I just. I never had that. And I need you to respect my time and not get upset when it seems like I forgot about you because I didn't. I don't. Sometimes I lose track of things, but…"

"Look, Mom, I'm sorry about smashing your cake. I overreacted. It won't happen again. When I get home, I'll stick to my room as usual, and you won't even know I'm there."

Her mom could be heard shuffling some papers in the background. "Right. Okay. Well, I look forward to having you home again. I've missed you."

I doubt it.

"Yeah, miss you too," Chloe forced out. "See you in a couple weeks."

Chloe hung up and slid the phone into her back pocket. As she neared the hill with the Kirk mansion atop, she tried to imagine the route Alexander would've taken. She looked from the stairs and then back toward where they found his body. Then she looked from the street to his driveway. Emma said the same model of Kia that Kevin drove was seen at his house just before Alexander would have left for his walk.

Chloe took her binoculars out of her bag and zoomed in. She saw Jared's car drive down the long driveway. The police had managed to gather more proof after searching Chad's house in B.C., which meant Jared had to fly out there to testify to the conversation he had heard, not that it was likely to stand in court.

Just as she was about to lower her binoculars, she caught a flash of silver through a thicket of trees further down the road. It passed Jared's car and was headed straight for the Kirk mansion.

Chloe dropped the binoculars in the sand and fumbled for her phone, hands shaking as she dialed Granny Em's number.

Chapter Thirty-Three

Emma was sitting on the back steps facing her garden when her phone began to ring.

"Hey, Chloe, need me to pick you up?"

"The Kia." She sounded breathless. "It's at the Kirks'. The same Kia. Amber she's…"

Emma jumped to her feet. "Whatever you do, stay put! Call Henry and tell him you saw some suspicious activity at the Kirk mansion, and he needs to check it out. I'll text you his cell."

Emma hung up and quickly copied and pasted Henry's number into the text message. She knew it would be better for Chloe to call the police directly, but she also knew if Chloe was truthful, they'd likely just laugh at her. Henry probably would laugh too, but he was a friend, and even if he thought her crazy, she knew he'd probably come check it out if only to save face.

Emma grabbed her keys out of her pocket and ran to the truck.

Tim, who was in the garden, ran over and grabbed the door just before she could close it.

"You wait for me," he ordered, rushing over to the passenger side.

Emma didn't even wait for him to buckle himself before she reversed at full force, turned and then raced out of the parking lot toward Amber's.

"Chloe said she saw that silver Kia drive up Kirk's driveway just moments ago."

"Did she call the cops?"

"They'd just laugh at her. There's no crime in someone driving up a driveway." She took a sharp turn, nearly sending Tim crashing against his window.

"Golly, you drive like my mother did."

Emma breathed a laugh. He *would* still be making jokes at this time. "I just need to get there."

Tim winced at the sound of the engine revving. "This might not be an emergency. Going at this speed could get you arrested, or worse, kill someone."

Emma slowed down just a little. She was almost at Amber's anyway. At least all the lights had been green on the way.

Tim looked out at the mansion closing in. "You let me go in. You stay put, okay?"

"Not a chance."

"Emma." His tone was sharp.

She sighed. "You can come in with me."

Tim didn't seem too pleased with this compromise, but he likely knew it was his best bet. "Fine."

Emma parked as close to the front door as possible. When she got out, she spotted the Kia conspicuously parked near the bushes.

As Emma neared the front steps, she noticed the front door was left slightly ajar.

"Stay quiet," she whispered to Tim.

"And you stay behind me," he hissed, stepping in front of her and holding his hand protectively up.

At first glance, everything looked as it always had, but then Emma heard multiple voices down the hall, toward the kitchen.

"What are you doing in my house?" She could hear Amber's shrill voice ring out. "How did you get in?"

Keys jingled. "Easy when you have a spare key." It was Julia's voice. What was she doing here?

Was she trying to get a confession out of Amber, or had she snuck in looking for clues and was now caught red-handed?

"So, you're the one my husband was sneaking into the house when he thought I was sound asleep?" Emma could practically hear Amber's eyes roll to the back of her head. "He was such an idiot to think I wouldn't notice—in my own house, of all places!"

"So, you knew?"

"Of course I knew. I heard you leave in a frenzy the morning of his death, yelling at him to leave me already. You were louder than a foghorn."

"You knew he loved me, and you kept him stuck?"

"He made his vows to me, not you. I was waiting for him to come to his senses. Ever since his honourable discharge from the navy, he was never the same. I figured this was just some midlife crisis or something, a phase. And let's be honest, dear, he probably didn't love either one of us. I certainly didn't force him to stay."

The voices stalled for a moment as Julia began to sniffle. "How could you say that? How could you?" Then there was angry crying.

Emma texted Henry: *'Where are you? Someone broke into Amber's home, and they are engaging in a heated conversation about Alexander. Door's unlocked.'*

Henry texted back: *'I've just pulled in.'*

"What are you waiting for?" Tim asked.

"A clue," Emma whispered back. "Maybe something will come to light through this."

"They're just fighting like cats over a dead man," he whispered back.

Emma was about to respond, but then Julia's angry voice distracted her.

"He did love me. He did. You might never believe it, but I know he did. He had an image to uphold. He was a man of power and wealth. He couldn't just leave. You—you could've made it easier for him." A loud sob erupted from Julia's lips.

Henry came up behind Emma at that moment. "What are you waiting for?" he whispered.

Emma held up a hand.

"You could've helped him to think rationally," Julia continued through her sobs, "so that—that I wouldn't have had to kill him."

Henry's eyes widened.

"You what?" Amber screeched. "You-you killed my husband?"

"I didn't mean to. I didn't want to. I had wanted to kill *you*. But that morning, after our fight, I chased after him. I grabbed the gun he had carelessly left on his desk. I didn't know why at the time. I wasn't thinking. I was so done. So done."

"But-but why? Why did you do it?" Amber's intonations went up and down. Emma could hear the tremble in her voice.

"He destroyed me. My marriage, my job—I lost everything to him. I couldn't find an ounce of happiness because of him. I hated him and I loved him all at once, and now—now I just hate you."

Henry slammed open the kitchen door and jumped into the scene. Emma was about to follow, but Tim held her back.

Julia was holding a gun now and pointing it at Amber.

"Put the gun down or I'll shoot." Henry's voice was firm.

Emma bit her lip, eyes glued to her friend's pale face and wide eyes. "It'll be okay," she mouthed.

The gun shook in Julia's grip.

"You don't want to do this," Henry said, his voice steady despite the tension crackling in the air.

"It isn't worth it. Killing her won't bring him back. And look around—you're surrounded by witnesses. There's no covering this up. If you don't lower the weapon, I'll have no choice but to shoot. So, tell me, Julia—what matters more? Revenge or your life?"

Julia's grip on the gun wavered. Her finger trembled against the trigger. For a breathless moment, Emma wasn't sure which way she'd go.

Then, slowly, her arm dropped. The weapon sagged in her grasp before she let it slip from her fingers.

She turned to Henry, her face hollow, eyes distant and unreadable. Then the dam broke. A choked sob tore from her throat, followed by another. Tears streamed down her cheeks, her lips quivering.

"I didn't mean to," she whispered. "I didn't—" Her words collapsed into strangled cries.

Henry moved quickly, securing the gun before clicking the cuffs around her wrists.

"You're under arrest," he said, his tone firm.

"So strange," Emma said as Henry shut the door of the squad car, sealing Julia inside. She folded her arms, staring after the woman who, only moments ago, had been on the brink of committing another murder.

"Chloe swore she overheard a conversation between Julia and Susan where Julia tried to pin the murder on her husband. She was adamant Alexander wouldn't have killed himself. And she even reached out to me, dropping hints that Chad was responsible. And now...she confesses?"

Henry exhaled, rubbing his jaw. "It's not uncommon in crimes of passion. The mind twists things, tries to justify, even rewrites reality. Maybe she knew, deep down, that foul play would be obvious and was only trying to throw us off her trail. Or maybe she was trying to convince herself of a lie.

Who knows?" He placed an arm on Emma's shoulder. "I owe you an apology. All along, you were right. There was a murderer in our midst."

Chapter Thirty-Four

Amber sat beside Emma in the sand, gazing out over the lake. The water shimmered under the moonlight, calm and unbothered—so unlike the storm that Emma knew was still raging inside her friend.

"I can't believe she murdered him," Amber said, her voice unsteady. "And that she tried to murder me." A shudder ran through her, and she hugged herself.

Emma exhaled, shaking her head. "I know. If I hadn't overheard that conversation, I don't know if I ever would've figured it out. I had my suspicions, but I kept assuming it had to be one of the men. I thought sabotage like that—it had to be a man's doing."

Amber swiped at a stray tear. "Well, Chad wasn't innocent either. Neither was my husband. Cutting corners, ignoring safety procedures—for what? I'll never understand." She forced a small, brittle smile. "Guess you solved more than one mystery, Miss Holmes."

Emma laughed and nudged her. "Not really. I just stumbled across the right clues. And honestly, Chloe did just as much work as I did."

Amber nodded. "She's leaving tomorrow, right?"

Emma swallowed hard and rubbed her throat, trying to will away the ache creeping in. "Yeah. I'll miss her. Being around her… it let me relive a little bit of motherhood."

Amber turned to her, eyes soft with understanding. "We all make mistakes as parents. No one teaches you how to do it right. All we have are our own parents' missteps burned into our memories more than anything good they did. But you love her, Emma. That's as obvious as the sun in the sky. She'll see it someday. And if she doesn't—well, plenty of people love you."

Emma smiled, resting her chin on her knees. "I know. And I love you all, too."

A warm breeze drifted through Chloe's open window, carrying the distant caw of seagulls and the rhythmic clapping of waves. She pulled her knees to her chest, her gaze falling to the messy pile of clothes still sitting in her unopened suitcase.

She didn't want to leave. She loved it here—even the musty scent from the drawers had grown on her, and so had her grandmother. Granny Em was the mother she had always wanted. Chloe wasn't invisible to her. She was seen and loved; that much she was certain of.

She dreaded leaving all this and going back to her mother, who was probably still mad at her.

A soft knock sounded at her door. "It's me," Granny Em called.

"Come in," Chloe said. "I'm just packing."

Granny Em stepped inside and looked at the suitcase, its contents stacked haphazardly on top of each other. She smirked. "You're not going to be able to zip that up."

Chloe shrugged. "I'll fold it, eventually."

Granny Em knelt beside the suitcase and started taking each item of clothing into her lap and folding it with perfect precision. "I know it's hard," she said. "I'll miss you more than words can say." Her bottom lip quivered, but she silenced it with a smile. "I'll call you every day if you want."

Chloe hugged her knees to her chest. "Thanks, I'd like that."

"And you can come visit for Christmas break. It's pretty dead around here during that time, so I'll have a lot of free time. We could actually do a little sightseeing."

"Yeah, I'd like that."

Granny Em crawled forward and wrapped her arms around Chloe. "You mean the world to me, Chloe. I love you. I'm so glad we've been able to spend this time getting to know each other better. You are beautiful inside and out and smart as a whip."

Granny Em pulled back and caught a tear sliding down Chloe's cheek. "Maybe when you return, there'll be another mystery to solve," she said with a wink.

Chloe laughed through her tears, swiping at her nose with her sleeve. "Maybe." Then her smile faltered. "At least Julia's been arrested. But it sounds like Chad's getting off scot-free. Not enough evidence to hold up in court—at least, from what Mike's been able to dig up."

"The world's not perfect," Granny Em said. "But justice always finds a way."

Chloe smirked and nudged her. "And the truth is bound to come out with Detective Ems on the case."

Granny Em cupped Chloe's cheek, warmth shining in her eyes. "Only with my sidekick's help."

The End.

Also by this Author:

KILLER IN THE MARGINS

I'M JESSICA LARSEN. MY MOM'S A POWERHOUSE ENTREPRENEUR, MY SISTER'S A DOCTOR, AND I'M... AN AUTHOR WITH A NORMAL 9-TO-5 THAT I CAN'T SEEM TO KEEP. AFTER GETTING FIRED (AGAIN) AND DUMPED BY MY BOYFRIEND OF TWO YEARS (AGAIN), I HAVE NO CHOICE BUT TO TAKE A JOB AS A CARETAKER FOR MY ECCENTRIC GRANDFATHER IN A TINY TOWN WITH NOTHING TO DO.

AT LEAST I'LL HAVE TIME TO WRITE—UNLESS, OF COURSE, I GET ROPED INTO SOMETHING RIDICULOUS.

like bonding with my grandfather over his secret past as a detective. Or stumbling onto a murder way too close to home.

Now, with my grandfather's old case files and a town full of quirky suspects, I have to solve this mystery—because surely, it can't be that different from writing crime novels... right?

Eliza Floretta writes fantasy books under the name Cara Ruegg. You can find more about those books at: https://cararueggauthor.com/

About the Author

Eliza Floretta writes cozy mysteries with heart, blending small-town charm, intriguing mystery, and characters you can't help but root for. Her stories follow determined heroines who unravel secrets, solve crimes, and sometimes find love along the way.

Outside of writing novels, she's a devoted wife and mother. She enjoys spending her time out in sunshine by a beach or in the forest.

She greatly appreciates her readers!

You are welcome to connect with her on social media. You can find her on Tiktok and Instagram as

@ElizaFloretta_author and on Facebook as Author Eliza Floretta.

If you enjoy a fantasy read with kisses only, she writes fantasy books under the name: Cara Ruegg

Printed in Dunstable, United Kingdom